SOLOMON PRO ATHLETES

No More Sidelines

Top-Scoring Player

Tap Out

RELAY PUBLISHING EDITION, DECEMBER 2022
Copyright © 2022 Relay Publishing Ltd.

Leslie North is a pen name created by Relay Publishing for co-authored Romance projects. Relay Publishing works with incredible teams of writers and editors to collaboratively create the very best stories for our readers.

Cover Design by Mayhem Cover Creations.

www.relaypub.com

SOLOMON PRO ATHLETES | BOOK TWO

USA TODAY BESTSELLING AUTHOR

LESLIE NORTH

BLURB

A perfect shot for romance fans…

NBA star Chase Holbrook's reputation with women is as legendary as his skill on the court. But when his affairs seem poised to distract him from the game, Chase accepts a team bet to steer clear of women for the season. Shouldn't be a problem for the ultra-competitive Chase — until the team's annoyingly cute team mascot is tasked with monitoring his every move.

Team mascot Willow "Bolt" Bend has always been one of the guys. So it's no surprise when she's asked to help ensure the integrity of the bet. Willow doesn't want to get involved, but her hesitation is sidelined by her desire to learn if Chase is as shallow as she thinks. All she has to do is keep an eye on the smoking hot player, and cry foul if he makes a move…

This perky mascot definitely knows how to get under Chase's skin. But with the bet well underway, Chase starts to see Willow in a whole new light. And as the sparks between them ignite, Chase begins to wonder if this is one bet he'll be happy to lose…

MAILING LIST

Thank you for reading "Top-Scoring Player"
(Solomon Pro Athletes Book Two)

Get FIVE full-length romances by USA Today best-selling author Leslie North for FREE! Over 900+ pages of best-selling romance with hundreds of FIVE STAR REVIEWS!

Sign-up to her mailing list and get your FREE books: www. leslienorthbooks.com/sign-up-for-free-books

CONTENTS

1

———

C hase Holbrook stepped to the free throw line.

About damned time.

Both teams were slow to assemble on the lane markers. One minute left, blowout by his team, the Pittsburgh Alloys. Most of the fans were already fleeing for their cars before slushy, late-season snow flew. The 19,000-seat arena was a near ghost town.

All game, he had argued with the refs for not calling Tennyson's flagrant fouls. The Raptors' golden boy, Tennyson, was the LeBron of Hogtown, which wasn't saying much. Anyone with a little game and a desire to make big free-agency bucks could be the cream that rose to the top of the league's worst team. Tennyson brought a thug mentality and little regard for where his body crashed down from the boards. Chase knew. His right arm and instep had intimate knowledge of the guy's elbows, knees, and testicles for the past forty court minutes.

Salty sweat drizzled past his lips. His right arm tweaked. Chase drilled his signature five dribbles into the varnished wood at his feet and planted his toes. Like any other shot he'd done a million times.

Like any other net-only shot that made the sweetest sound hushing through the rim mics and made him the most upwardly mobile offensive player in the NBA. Like any other free throw in his streak of thirty-eight no misses.

A carpi muscle in his forearm seized; the ball's leather slipped from his slick grip.

The ball reacted as if he were a grandmother with arthritis who had shot with her bunions.

His stomach dropped to his nuts.

Total fucking air ball.

Chants rose from the Raptors fans behind the goal.

"Aiiiiiirrrrr ballllll…Aiiiiiiiirrrr balllll."

Muttering out a fuck you on the close-up camera angles of a national broadcast network wasn't an option. Chase was nothing if not a gracious player. He lifted a diminutive, almost celebratory, hand as if to say "my bad" and flashed his smile that always boded well for his alt-career, modeling. His point guard, Tarek, kept a tally reminiscent of *It's a Wonderful Life*: Every time Holbrook smiled at the camera, ten thousand women lost their panties. Inside, however, he stewed. Tennyson should have been ejected for the latest hit. The shot should have been ruled a technical.

Chase swiped his palms on the ass of his shorts and set his second shot.

"Aiiiiiirrrrr ballllll…Aiiiiiiiirrrr balllll," taunted the crowd. Damned if it wasn't some fans in Pitt's blue and gold, too. So much for loyalty. A smattering of noisemakers and red and black wiggle sticks snagged his attention but only for a moment.

He made a deal with the rim, dribbled five, and released.

Swish.

Coach called a time out to put in rookies. A cacophony of referee whistles sounded.

At the bench, Chase returned Tarek's discrete hand smack. Not his fucking grin. The shit storm of smack talk for that missed shot would be relentless. He toweled off his face, tuned out the coach's game plan for the rookies. Having taken them to a twenty-six-point lead, what he'd put up by halftime, he had earned the right to check out early.

Thing was, what was left of the crowd wasn't checking out early. Fan noise swelled, signaling something other than the dry, competition-less play that had dominated the second half. Tarek nudged Chase's elbow. He followed Tarek's line of attention to the free throw line Chase had just evacuated.

The Alloy's mascot, Bolt, wiggled its…whatever…psycho-furry black ass with an embellished bump-and-grind hardly appropriate for a beaver-panther-lunatic hybrid and the ten-year-olds left in the crowd and took a shot.

An exaggerated air ball.

The remaining fans howled. Berserk with laughter. Loudest they'd been in thirty minutes of play. Even Tarek gave an appreciative clap.

Perfect. Just ripe.

Chase's face steamed off its sweat.

Bolt made a grand gesture of bowing to all four directions in the stands. The traitorous ref bounce-passed the game ball back to the mascot. Bolt lined up for another free throw, did four rump-shakers back past the three-point arc, turned and took a backwards granny shot.

Swish.

The crowd roared and rose to their feet. Chase had put up thirty-eight points in the game and this roadkill gets the noise.

"Why they stay, baby," said Tarek, grinning ear to ear. "Genius."

Chase didn't think it was genius at all. In fact, he fucking hated mascots. Most of the time they were creepy and made kids cry. He dropped into his court-side seat, his eyes burning a hole in the side of the costume's head as it made its way off the wood behind the north glass, high-fiving anyone within reach. It wasn't the first time Bolt had ripped him on the court, but it sure as hell would be the last.

At the end-of-game buzzer, he went straight for the Alloy's tunnel where he'd seen the fuzzy goon disappear. No media interviews. No words of encouragement for the rooks that just finished the team strong. Nothing but a score to settle that had zero to do with basketball.

He caught sight of the mole-like, fox-like backside padding into the restricted hallway to the locker room, still high-fiving—staffers in blue and gold polos, Alloy players, trainers, even the chef responsible for keeping them all sleek and happy. Chase jogged faster and caught up to Bolt just as the helmet-head lifted clear of the inside body.

Hand clamped on the costume's hairy shoulder, Chase stopped the mascot's progress to the inner labyrinth.

The perky little gymnast inside, with the pig-tails and a wad of green gum snapping between her molars, blinked back her surprise.

"'Sup, Holbrook?"

"The fuck was that?"

Her pixie face contorted into a mask of pity. "Looked like a whiff to me, stud. Bad one, at that. Probably make the ESPN lead story: Worst shots in NBA history."

Chase gnashed his teeth. "I meant your little show out there."

"Great shot, wasn't it?" Tarek smacked Chase on the back before engaging in a rehearsed and rather intricate celebratory dance with mascot girl. Whatever the hell her name was. "Check you later, sweet thing."

Tarek rejoined the tide of Alloy players streaming toward the locker room.

Mascot girl beamed a perfect row of miniature teeth. Until she turned back to Chase. She rolled her eyes and removed the remainder of her costume, bouncing and writhing in a magnificent display of sweat and inept undressing. And zero tits. Whatsoever.

"No more singling me out, you hear? I can have you fired faster than you can squeeze out of that—whatever the hell it is—costume."

"It's a muskrat," she rallied, confidently, before her brows twisted and her gaze crumbled. "I think."

"It's hideous, and it smells like vomit and sweaty balls on the inside."

She took an exaggerated whiff, all grin and flared, petite nostrils. "Kinda like your career if you don't get that free throw under control. The fans love me. The owner loves me. I'm sorry if your fragile ego doesn't feel the same. I forgive you for the threat. I'd kiss you to prove it if I didn't smell like sweaty balls. Night, Holbrook."

On her way past him, dragging the furry carcass, she blew him a kiss and tossed him a wink.

He'd lost count of the number of times Bolt had blown him kisses this season, usually right after some mocking little routine. On national TV.

"What kind of crappy mascot makes fun of the home team players?"

She stopped short and tipped her head to the side. "I don't make fun of all of you. Just the special ones." Her *special* smacked of sarcasm.

"What the hell did I ever do to you?"

"Hello…*GQ* interview? Playoffs, last season? Ring a bell?"

"No."

"You said, and I quote, 'the current mascot is only entertaining to kids and the mentally challenged.'"

Chase smirked, a fresh wave of appreciation for the quote washing over him. "I did say that."

"There's nothing funny about that. You alienated an entire group of people who already have enough struggles in life. Not to mention, it isn't true." She lifted her chin, a weak show of righteousness. "Everyone loves Bolt."

He shook his head, wishing it were as easy to shake this irritating girl from his space.

"Stay away from me. Pretend I don't exist on the court."

"Shouldn't be too hard since you're more famous for your mattress skills than your game skills."

For a fraction of a second, he considered ripping the costume away from her and shredding it with his hands. Would assaulting the fake muskrat pelt be a violation of the league's code of conduct? He resisted the urge—he had to take a monster leak and simply no longer had the energy to match her word-for-word.

He made a beeline for the locker room.

"Holbrook?"

He paused and squeezed his eyelids shut, braced himself for her next insult. He refused to give her the satisfaction of turning around.

"Great game. Thirty-eight is two better, right?"

Her voice was new, quieter in the thinning tunnel crowd, wholly sincere. His instinct told him to nod, acknowledge the compliment in some way. But he was fast learning with a crazy wildcard like her, a millimeter given would turn into a fast break the length of a court. He lifted his jersey collar, rubbed the sweat from his lashes and continued on to the locker room where he showered, dressed, and said his good-byes to his squad, every one of whom had grown to expect the performance he exhibited against the Raptors.

Appreciation ran in short supply by this stage of the season.

As it turned out, Bolt girl was the only one the rest of the night to mention that he had blown past his personal scoring record.

2

———

Washing Bolt was a three-hour endeavor: removing the wire structures, using industrial washing machines and low-heat dry cycles, and then going through a grooming routine that would shame a Hollywood starlet. The ones that Chase Holbrook dated, with their airbrushed skin and rehearsed pouts that made them look more constipated than sexy. But Willow wouldn't trade this gig for nearly anything.

Except maybe a gig with Gordon Ramsay. Guy was all food and testosterone. Yum.

As usual, she padded barefoot back onto the Alloy's empty court and worked on her routine while Bolt tumbled, floppy ears over tail, through the laundry cycles. With back-to-back home games, she needed to work out the spacing of the trampolines for her next half-time show so she didn't make the highlight reels for the wrong reasons.

She caught sight of Tarek as he was leaving, a duffle large enough to smuggle a body tossed over his shoulder. He hugged her, despite him being freshly showered and smelling like a hot cabana boy and her smelling like—well, sweaty balls, apparently.

"Did your mom try that Australian cream on her joints?" she asked.

"Loves it. She wanted me to thank you. Says they can't smell her coming now at Wednesday choir practice."

"She's a classy Southern lady. She should smell like magnolia, not menthol."

"Need a ride?"

"Not finished yet. Walt said he'd stay and lock up after me. I brought him lasagna."

"You still need to cook for me. When's that gonna happen?"

She didn't want to admit she no longer had a kitchen. As of yesterday, she had been evicted and was living on the couch of her mother's eighty-one-year-old friend. Estelle needed Willow's money more than that crooked landlord, anyway. He didn't need pills to keep his heart beating—if he ever had a heart.

"My kitchen is cramped." Not a lie. Metamucil bottles everywhere. "A true Cajun feast requires space."

"I got nothing but space, sweet thing. After our next jog out to the west coast."

"Deal."

Tarek took a few steps toward the exit, then turned back. "Hey, how's your nephew?"

"Treatments are just holding back the inevitable. Buying him time. He's still begging me for the chance to meet Holbrook. I don't see what Dylan idolizes in him. Guy is nothing but ego in size fourteen shoes."

"Chase is…"

"Narcissistic?" she offered.

Tarek smiled.

"Conceited?"

He shook his head.

"Grouchy and promiscuous?"

A sharp guffaw lit Tarek's expression. "Aren't those things mutually exclusive?"

"Not when you look like an Adonis in track shorts."

"I was going to say misunderstood," said Tarek. "None of us are really our persona. You should get to know him."

"I know all I need to know. Dylan is the kindest soul on the planet. He shouldn't have to find out that his hero is a jerk. He can't endure one more disappointment in his young life."

"Disappointment is one word I would never use in the same sentence with Chase Holbrook."

"Killer jump shots don't count."

"I'm not talking about on the court." Tarek continued on toward the exit and pointed at her for emphasis. "Great stuff out there tonight, W. Really funny."

"Later."

When Tarek wasn't calling her sweet thing, he called her W, more like dubbya with his faint Louisiana drawl. Made her feel a bit like a kindred spirit to the forty-third president. Or a badass superhero. From the moment she took over Bolt from Ned Lehrman because he wanted to climb Mount Everest—and a cougar from Italy, in that order—

Tarek and the rest of the guys had welcomed her like a little sis. But Chase had never been part of that. He had been traded from Sacramento two years later with all the mystery and fanfare of royalty. Royalty with an underwear contract rumored to be close to sixty million. For sixty mil, she'd *eat* underwear. Imagine the network of pay-it-forward restaurants that sum would open.

She worked her routine until Bolt was dry and Walt got antsy. He had a hot number at the bingo hall—Dottie—who was as slow to warm up as a diesel engine and who fizzled out fast. By midnight, all bets were off. Willow doubted Walt's security guard prowess. Many late nights exiting the arena, she believed her brief stint with *Murder Those Buns* and its companion DVD, *Slay Those Abs*, might serve them both better than his shaky hand on a pistol. But he had been private, first-class Army and a member of Pittsburgh's finest for thirty years. He deserved every ounce of chivalry between them.

At Estelle's place, she showered and flopped on a floral-print velour sofa that looked as if it had been resurrected from the *Golden Girls* television set. During a caught-cheating hidden-camera show, a commercial for Magnum underwear came on. Chase's abs, so very fine in every way, slid across the screen. The ad was tastefully artsy in black and white, with gaunt supermodels sporting vacuous stares. Willow pressed the back button on the DVR remote and watched it again before she caught herself looking for the rumored millisecond-slippage of the camera angle below his designer-stamped equator.

Nada.

Pillow pressed over her head as punishment, she growled. No way she would sleep anytime soon. She baked four pans of blackberry-walnut cake bars for the smack-down bake sale Estelle's WWF Catholic charities group, Women Worshipping Fabulously, was having. While they were in the oven, she mopped the kitchen floor and whipped through the dishes. Helping out around the house—cooking, cleaning, keeping

Estelle company—was her rent, in her mind. Her way of paying the older woman back for letting Willow crash on her sofa until she figured out her life.

Willow hoped a plan materialized soon. She couldn't help others if she couldn't even help herself.

After morning shoot arounds, Chase felt ambushed.

His teammates crowded the Alloys locker room. Free to shower, work out, chow down or leave, they lingered for the sole purpose of witnessing the continuing banter Tarek had begun with Chase on the upstairs court moments before. Chase simply stared at the wall of television screens showing NBA highlights from the late west coast games the previous night.

Tarek knew Chase wouldn't talk about the women he dated—never had since back in his Kings days—but that didn't stop Tarek from trying to loosen up a few golden nuggets of gossip when Chase's name or mug hit the news cycle.

"Come on, bruh. They linked you with Chrissy La Roux. Caught you coming out of her set trailer on location up north."

Chase shook his head. "Grainy photo. Wasn't me."

"How many other lanky white dudes she keep around her?" Tarek made a disgusted little tsk-grunt sound as he peeled off his shirt. "Chrissy. La Roux." He dragged her name out as if it needed any more emphasis.

She was a fiery five-foot-five, redheaded bombshell Hollywood A-lister. *People* magazine cover, daily TMZ A-lister. That particular pap shot was from one of Chase's less discreet moments last off-season that he regretted to this day. The press seemed hell-bent on putting them together. Chase, however, was hell-bent on shattering the NBA's offensive scoring record.

With the Alloys largely out of the playoffs due to a young, inexperienced lineup behind him and Tarek, the offensive award was still noteworthy and within reach. Silencing dating gossip was one thing. But silencing the collective press who filled the sports squawk shows with the prevailing opinion that Chase had been overpaid in the Kings trade, wasn't worth his hype, and couldn't get the job done for Pittsburgh was a far richer ambition. Some pro players were lauded for their defense, their electricity on the court, their sportsmanship. Chase could drain. Simple as that. Nothing fancy, just consistent. So he vowed to keep his head down, his mind on the game, and drain buckets until no one could touch him.

Not even Tarek.

Chase looked over at his tightest competition for the offensive honor and his damned near best friend. Closest thing to a brother Chase had besides Marcus and Henry—the guys he'd grown up with, training at Solomon's gym. But even Tarek wasn't close enough to penetrate Chase's inside world of hungry expectations, detached relationships, and quests to prove himself. Most nights, his drive was what kept him awake, not the advances of a beautiful woman.

"Don't believe it. Chasing the gold, leaving your ass in the dust, has me celibate. No women until that award is mine." Chase tossed his sweaty practice jersey into the laundry bin.

"Not this celibate shit again, man. All that shit about not getting any making your game better is a myth. A mental hang-up. You'd be better off climbing up to the top of the Comcast building, pulling down your shorts, and waiting for a unicorn to fly up your ass. More likely, too, given the women who orbit your second-place butt."

Rogers, the rookie small forward with an unparalleled appreciation for the game's history, chimed in. "Wilt Chamberlain swore by it."

"Lies, bruh. He never had a celibate stretch in his career," Tarek said. "Let's just say Wilt the Stilt wasn't called The Big Dipper for having to lower his head to pass through doorways. He tapped half of Pennsylvania in his day. Probably Booth's mother."

Booth beamed at Tarek. "After which your mother got sloppy seconds."

A chorus of ooooohs and declarations of owning filled the locker room. Chase laughed, relieved the smack talk had veered away from him. The comradery on this team was unparalleled. Chase may have been late to the game, starting at sixteen, but he'd been on teams year round for twelve years and had never felt such genuine warmth from his teammates. Ever.

"Science proves it," said Nunzio, their teddy bear center with the Kid 'n Play afro. "Study out of Cornell or some shit. No sex leads to peak performance. Brains, body, all that shit."

"That's jacked," said Tarek. "It's like playing constipated. Ain't nothing magic flowing outta those fingertips when all systems aren't firing."

"Spurs made a celi-bet in '14," said Wilcox, a power forward covered in tats. "Ask me how that worked out for us." Wilcox never failed to remind them he played for San Antonio that season—though played was a relative term; his position had been bench warmer.

"You telling me you won the championship that year because ain't none of you got laid?" Booth said.

"I can't speak for the others, but the bet was a unifying piece of the puzzle."

"Man, you just didn't get any because of that red nappy-ass hair," said Tarek. "Ain't no bet to blame there."

Again, more congratulatory smack-down hand slaps.

"I declare it's time to start our own unifying tradition," said Nunzio. "Holbrook's already in."

"Ain't no championship on our horizon," said Booth. "Tarek and Holbrook only ones with a shot at glory this season."

Never one to back down from a challenge, which was the primary reason Tarek was all over Chase's tail for Offensive Player of the Year, Tarek turned to Chase. "How 'bout it. You and me. A celi-bet. A unifying piece of the puzzle."

"Nah," said Chase. "Bets are a distraction. I got to focus."

"Then what better way, my friend, than to ensure you're at your peak performance. That is, unless you think it's bullshit, too."

Chase knew it wasn't. For his NCAA streak his senior year at Iowa and the mid-season run for the Alloys last year, the strategy had worked for him. His gaze drifted over to the television screens where he caught a flash of the photo taken of him and Chrissy at the red carpet premiere of last year's summer blockbuster. If anything, the bet was performance insurance. And if there was anything he liked less than dating gossip, it was losing a bet to Tarek.

"Terms?" asked Chase.

They both looked to Wilcox, resident expert on such matters.

Wilcox shrugged. "No sex until one of you breaks the NBA scoring record, or the season ends. First one to cave loses the bet."

"Define sex," said Tarek.

Sixteen other players chimed in various explanations of penetration, dry humping, double penetration, hand jobs, oral, anal. The discussion devolved until someone made a Bill Clinton joke about what *is* meant. They decided on the clinical definition of intercourse—vagina and penis—though Chase had no intention of allowing any woman near his junk. Any release of testosterone defeated the purpose.

"How much money?" shouted Booth.

"Let's make it interesting, shall we? Holbrook has all that tighty-whities cash." Tarek paced for show then stopped for a grand announcement. "Ten thousand dollars."

A few whistles, some gasps. This amount seemed to impress those gathered. Chase had this locked. Guaranteed win.

Chase extended his hand. "You're on."

Tarek's brows rose. He shook Chase's hand to seal the bet. "Prepare to go down, Magnum."

"Wait," said Nunzio. "How are we going to know?"

"Bet monitors. To be with the player when he's not with the team," offered Wilcox. "Each of you names a bet monitor for the other. It's the only fair way."

Chase saw the perfect opportunity to pay Tarek back for the time he'd enlisted the Suns' owner to prank him during a charity event, informing him he'd been cut from the Alloys and asking if he would like to try out for Phoenix's D-league. Chase could name one of his supermodel contacts to tempt Tarek, but the truth was, Tarek was in love with the one who got away, still hoping they'd get back together. If there was a chance they'd work it out, Chase wanted no part of endangering that. The perfect solution materialized. Forget celibacy. Challenge Tarek's sanity.

"I name your mother."

Tarek slid out a curse and paced away. Guy was always on the move. Even more so when he was riled about something.

More love from the spectators—hoots, hollers, laughter. Booth did a special dance-move out of his nook to high-five Chase. When the celebration quieted, their heads all turned to Tarek in anticipation of his chosen bet monitor.

Tarek's eyes squinted; his lips pursed in thought.

Chase's stomach soured like he'd run lines for a half-hour after eating a four-course meal.

"C'mon, man," said Nunzio when the verdict was too slow. "Out with it."

"Willow Bend."

Wait, was that a street? Tarek was trolling him. Chase's thoughts backlogged amidst the equally-festive commentary surrounding them. Booth danced over to Tarek and shared another high-five. Apparently, everyone knew something—or someone—Chase didn't.

"Who?"

"Mascot girl," offered Nunzio.

Chase's awareness slammed back to the tunnel after last night's game where the sweaty-balls girl in pigtails insulted his free throw, his intelligence, and his reputation, all within the span of a minute.

"No. No, no, no."

"What you mean 'no'? If there was a no option here, don't you think I would have used it on my mama? Woman never met a locked door she didn't bust her way through."

"Not Bolt girl. She has it out for me."

"Then you don't gotta worry about banging her," said Wilcox. "Record's yours."

"She'll never agree to it," said Chase, determined to hunt down any excuse to make this not happen. Forget celibacy. This was his sanity at stake.

"You gotta make her agree. Or you can just lay out the ten-grand now." Tarek mimed an ego-filled show-me-the-money pose, complete with a fingertip lick and a Cheshire smile.

Chase glanced around at the smug faces of his teammates. No way he was parting a bet within a minute. He picked up a nearby basketball and drilled five crisp dribbles into the carpeted Alloy's logo. On the court, this made the world drop away. In here, sixteen sets of eyes on him made the world more crowded than a capacity playoff game.

"You're going down, Tarek."

He dropped the ball and headed for the weight room. Behind him, Nunzio's gravelly voice whipped the team into a frenzy with two words.

"Bet pool!"

3

———————

The next night, the Alloys beat the 76ers by three on home court. Hyper-focused for the in-state rivalry, Chase played his best game in recent memory—highly attuned to rebounding, blocking shots, and banging in the key. Everything beyond the first rim of courtside chairs ceased to exist. That included mascot girl.

Until it was time to leave.

Tarek's mother had already moved into his place and taken over his bathroom counter with anti-aging serums and home remedies for hot flashes. This shifted odds on the bet pool, with some Chase supporters upping their antes. His twenty-four hours to secure his bet monitor before he forfeited was almost up.

Chase, showered and dressed in his regulation warm-ups, emerged from the tunnel onto the court. Someone said he could find Bolt girl there long after the media cleared and the cleaning crews began. Arena lights were already half-strength, casting an odd glow on the varnished gold and blue floor and affording him a chance to blend in with the shadows.

He wasn't sure which held him back more—asking someone who had a clear distaste for him to move in and ensure he didn't have sex or the athletic exhibition she put on when she thought no one was looking. She was Sheryl Swoopes and a Globetrotter, all rolled into a gymnast's package: alley-oops, airborne twists, vaulted tomahawks. A few times she stumbled. Once, she landed ass-first on the padded mat then lay back and stared at the arena ceiling, her chest heaving. She wiped away the sweat from her brow, jogged back to mid-court and tried again. This time, she launched off the trampoline and executed a full-on 720 dunk.

Holy shit.

The flashiest shot Chase had ever done was a windmill. Even that dunk felt odd beneath his skin. He had always left showmanship to others. Sol's advice. Respect the game. Make it about the game. Always the game. Truth was, he wasn't sure he had anything but a dependable jumper in him, but he appreciated the athleticism required to pull off the shots that unhinged the crowd. Sure, she used a tramp to make up for her height deficiency, but she attacked the net with an authority that totally contradicted her name.

Willow.

She probably had hippie parents and wove macramé tunics on weekends with a name like that.

If he didn't ask, he couldn't get out of here and get some much-needed shut eye. He shifted the duffle hanging from his shoulder, savored a deep breath, and walked onto the court with zero prep as to what he would say. Repaying her lone compliment in their only other conversation seemed a good start. He snagged her attention as she was starting to break down the equipment.

"Impressive. Where'd you learn those mad skills?"

She blinked, taken aback for a heartbeat. He expected a smartass response. Instead, civility.

"Four older brothers and a lifetime of gymnastics."

"You do all that with a fifty-pound costume on?" He set down his bag and helped, carting the first trampoline off once she had folded its legs. For all that mascot girl lacked in the upstairs department, she more than made up on the lower floor. Her black athletic shorts shrink-wrapped an exquisite set of muscular glutes and legs. When she folded in half to do the heavy lifting, he nearly dropped his end looking at the inviting curve between her thighs.

He caught himself, horrified, and recalled her savage tongue. Mercifully, this cooled his jets.

"I try. If I miss, then it turns into comedy. Win-win either way."

"You ever miss?"

"Hawks last year. Somersault into the post."

Chase remembered that game. He didn't remember anything beyond his performance.

"Ouch."

"Luckily, Bolt has a pelt that smells like sweaty balls. Cushioned the blow."

He winced at her throwback to their previous argument. Best to change the subject.

"You always stay late like this?"

"I have to sneak in time before the event staff turns the floor for the Penguins."

Chase had never thought about it much, what happened after his job was over for the night. They once did a fundraiser for the floor manager whose daughter had leukemia. Hundreds showed up, a huge portion in staff gear. He'd been floored by how many people it took to run this place. He continued to help her break down the equipment until the last piece was secured. The lack of conversational direction grew as awkward as Chase trying not to notice her hard nipples through the Lycra of her sports bra.

She broke the silence. "I know you didn't stay to be chivalrous. That's Walt's job."

There was an insult in there, but Chase was too preoccupied with approaching his delicate subject to acknowledge. He decided direct was best. Mascot girl seemed to have a knack for bluntness.

"I need a favor."

"Ah, here it is." She zipped on an Alloy's hoodie and finished packing the rest of her gear into a messenger bag. "Only took you ten minutes to warm up. Kinda like your first quarter starts."

Veins in his neck throbbed. He shook his head and stalked away. "Forget it."

"Wait." She scrambled after him and snagged his elbow. The last thing he wanted to do was turn around. Mascot girl was like a menagerie—never knew what kind of animal or sideshow or crackpot comment you'd get. He'd never been so mystified by a woman. And not in a good way. He stalled his progress at her insistence and turned.

She offered him a stick of gum.

His brain went on shut down. He'd take Tarek's mother's age serums over Willow's randomness any day.

"Peace offering."

Definitely hippy parents. She unwrapped the foil overlay and made an appalling show of folding a too-big stick of gum against her tongue then slid a fresh piece out of the package for him.

"I'm sure pounding the court for forty minutes gives you breath that could knock over a water buffalo."

Chase couldn't attest to that. For the first time in a very long time, he felt self-conscious. He had stripped to nothing but cock socks for photo shoots and here he was, awkward over bad breath. He took the gum and slid it into his mouth.

"Continue." Although she was only as tall as his pecs, her cinnamon breath reached him on a spicy, warm cloud.

"It was Tarek's idea, really." That's right. Throw him under the bus for this. "We made a bet and he named you my bet monitor."

"What's that?"

"Someone to make sure we abide by the terms of the bet."

She blew an ambitious pink bubble. It bounced while her evocative tongue waggled inside. The snap almost made him jump.

"And my responsibilities?"

"You'd have to move in."

Her eyes bugged. "With you?"

"And be with me when the team isn't—which during the season isn't much."

"Until?"

"Until Tarek disqualifies himself or I break the league offensive scoring record."

"And how does Tarek disqualify himself from the bet?"

"He has sex."

The magnitude of the bet dawned in her speckled brown eyes. She rolled her eyes with a magnitude that would have flipped a ferry on the Allegheny.

"You made a celi-bet?"

"You've heard of those?"

"Who hasn't? Biggest load of crap in professional sports. Performance is not tied to sex drive. It's just a way for athletes with fragile egos to explain away incompetence and push misogynistic blame on the fairer sex."

Fantastic. A hippie and a feminist. He began mentally subtracting ten grand from his bank balance. No way he was living with this woman. His feet were already headed for the exit.

"Wait."

Chase stopped short.

"What's in it for me? Besides getting to see your smokin' hot body every day?"

Was this girl for real? No filter whatsoever. Still, he felt himself fucking flush.

"How much is the bet?" she asked.

He didn't want to say. The amount made him feel like an asshole with too much money.

"Ten grand."

She choked on her gum. Legitimately. Beet-faced and all. For a second, he thought he'd have to give her the Heimlich.

"That's a lot of underwear," she finally squeaked out.

"Not as much as you'd think." He couldn't help the slight smile that tried to twitch free. "Hold up your end, it's all yours. This isn't about the money. I just need someone to vouch for my free time and run interference on women."

"Groupies?"

Maybe it was the slight, suspicious angle she regarded him with or her devilish smirk. His smile loosened. "Some, maybe."

"Bitches be crazy. I'll earn every penny of that ten grand."

That's precisely what worried him.

"I value my privacy. We'll barely get in each other's way." He hoped.

"I have a life, you know."

"I practice here more than anyone. And we have an away game stretch coming up that gets you off the hook. Tarek will cave by then."

"Who's his monitor?"

"His mom."

Willow sucked in a breath through her teeth. Everyone, it seemed, was sympathetic toward Tarek's pain on that one. She nodded and popped another bubble.

"And you went along with me because I'm the least desirable woman you know?"

It was Chase's turn to choke, this time on her candor. His voice went on injured reserve.

"We're nothing if not honest, Holbrook. Admit that I'm safe because you'd never, ever have sex with me, and we'll move on."

His throat closed. This felt like one of those ghastly verbal snares laid by women to trap men into saying the wrong thing to prove a point.

She had nailed the truth, not because he didn't find her mildly appealing—her nipples and rock-hard ass, after all—but because he would never bed a woman that got under his skin like a bedbug and called him out on everything. He scrambled for something that didn't make him sound like a bigger asshole than the ten grand.

"Tarek said the arrangement would benefit us both. That's all."

There. Diplomatic. Somewhat truthful. And bringing Tarek back in didn't hurt. Tarek adored her. Everyone who knew Willow apparently adored her. Everyone but Chase.

"I'll consider it if you help me with something." She fished out a pair of black inline skates from her bag and began lacing them up.

"Now?"

"Won't take long." She stood and tested the rollers with a back-and-forth shimmy of her legs. "You skateboard?"

"Not since I was fourteen."

"Like riding a bike." She grabbed his wrist and led him up the closest arena aisle, surprisingly adept at rollers on stairs. "You'll see."

"Look—I gotta get home." He tugged back, striving for freedom from the most bizarre, highest-energy person he had ever met. Exhaustion burned his corneas. His custom pillow beckoned him. "Think about it. You can let me know in the morning."

Willow stopped her upward progress and turned. Her smallish lips did a quirky little twist, somewhere between a sexy pout and a frown that telegraphed extreme disappointment. He had already offered her ten grand. What the hell else did she want?

Above her head, a lit marquee scrolled past his field of vision.

...Tarek Johns – 32 points... Chase Holbrook – 34 points... Race to the record books.

Holbrook came alphabetically before Johns, and he had more game points. So why was he listed second? His gut ignited, the same burn that happened at tip off. Chase would win this bet, this record, even if it meant putting up with a whack-job girl in a muskrat costume.

"What do you want me to do?" asked Chase.

Absolute insanity.

He thought Willow had been kidding about the skateboard, but she went to a supply closet and pulled out a wide-deck with crazy pink dots and lime green wheels.

"Used it for a halftime gig once," she offered, by way of explanation, then shoved it into his hands with a conspiratorial smile. She grabbed another massive, empty cloth bag from the closet and took off. By the time he had looped his duffle cross-body, she had flown around the corner, out of sight.

"Where are you going?" Chase called after her. He tried to launch and failed. "What are we doing?"

"You'll see." Her disembodied voice bounded through the vacant hall.

He followed because he believed it to be the closest distance between this moment and his soft, ergonomically-programmable bed. His bag was entirely too heavy to catch any real speed, but the cleaning crew blasting old-school Metallica and the air blowing back his damp hair conspired to push him past his comfort level. Willow had been right—it was like riding a bike. Before long, he had regained enough confidence to know he wouldn't wipe out.

Coach Perkins's intestines would drop out through his bowels if he knew his lead scorer was risking injury, flying through the arena's circular concourse on a skateboard at breakneck speed. Down a straightaway, he caught sight of her at a concession stand, its cage rolled up halfway. She shoved wrapped burgers, boxed pizza slices, popcorn bags and clear take-out boxes that contained nachos drizzled with nuclear cheese into her empty cloth bag.

What the hell?

Before he could catch up to her, she blew a kiss to the guy behind the counter, yelled, "I'll bring the book tomorrow," and raced off. She stopped at no less than six snack bars, each with a staffer waiting with half-cage anticipation and a wide grin, each supplying her enough food for an entire row of the arena. He trailed her, wordless, baffled, nearly incensed that she would take advantage of the system this way. At the final concession stand, she had run out of room in her bag and started shoving hot dogs in warming sleeves into his hands.

"Favor done," he declared.

She pointed to the wieners. "That's not the favor."

Ohmygod. He was never, ever leaving here. The arena was The Twilight Zone and she was Rod Serling with pigtails. And nipples.

"Willow, I'm done." Chase shoved the plump foil sleeves into her hands, kicked the skateboard to his hand—impressed that he still had the goods for that particular move—and pulled his cell from his athletic shorts. He started a text to Tarek.

Rather live with your mother. Bet off.

Before he could hit send, Willow called out.

"Typical Holbrook. All talk, but can't put things away. Lakers, especially. Go then. Battle the broads on your own. Good luck with that."

Her voice was half-admonishment, half-tease, all irritating. She skated in reverse, her scammed stash like Santa's pack on her shoulders. Had to be at least the weight of Bolt's costume, maybe more. Would serve her right if she got a back ache.

"It isn't what you think, stud. Come on."

She shoved through the arena doors and disappeared out into the night.

Chase glanced at the vendor of the Nutty Norwegian Nut Stand, Willow's words echoing in the cavernous space. Isn't what you think. Come on…on…on. The round guy in the stained apron shrugged.

"I'm going to regret this," Chase said.

For a minute, Chase was convinced the blond spoke no English. Then he smiled, rammed the gate closed, and said, "Not likely. Stud."

Dude laughed and disappeared into a back room.

Menagerie. Chase glanced at his cell screen.

Rather live with your mother. Bet off.

He clicked off the phone and shoved it in his pocket. Skateboard back on the ground, he followed Willow out the arena doors on the sketchy advice of the Nutty Norwegian.

4

____

"Does it run?" Chase asked, doubtful.

"Of course it runs."

Willow's tone was defensive, as if the orange 1970s-era VW Bus at the center of the empty parking lot was her first-born, and he had just insulted the shape of its head. The opening ritual for the reluctant passenger door was a show in itself—two well-placed bangs on the outside, a hand-crank window roll from the inside, and a foot shove only a gymnast could appreciate.

"Get in. It's freezing," she said.

Not for the first time since the game, Chase questioned his judgment. Being with Willow was like boarding a swift-moving bullet train headed in the wrong direction: powerless to stop once it got going and mildly fascinating in a semi-nauseous kind of way. He expected the car to smell like Julius Erving's game sneakers after walking through a vat of curdled yogurt. Surprisingly, the air freshener spinning on the brisk wind they ushered into the car whirled up a sickeningly fruity-sweet scent. Until Willow planted her stale snack pack in his lap.

"You have a wagon. Can't we put this in the back?"

"Not efficient."

She focused her attention on starting the car. If the old VW's engine had a voice, it would have been an octogenarian with emphysema, gas and road rage all at once. Chase found himself holding his breath, as if his lack of oxygen could somehow inject the right amount of fuel or make him pass out in a bewildering haze of side stream fumes. Once her tongue slipped free of her lips in extreme concentration, the four-wheeled turd growled to life.

"Am I going to pass a random drug test after this?" Legit, he was worried.

"I'll have you know that this beaut was overseen by John DeLorean, himself. And the Kammback Panel Express edition offers an unparalleled level of privacy in the back."

"For stealing?" The food steaming his crotch was still impairing his thought process.

"For having sex. So no borrowing while the bet is on."

"No worries there."

She pulled out into the traffic streaming by the arena. The Bus hesitated, lurched, and misfired with the aplomb of a 9-millimeter gun.

Chase ducked.

"It does that on cold nights."

He wanted to tell her that air temperature had nothing whatsoever to do with fuel burning outside the combustion chamber, but he was too busy trying to maintain his post-game power bar in his stomach. Between the sour nacho cheese smell, the blue cloud from the back-fire, and her Mario Andretti driving, he barely had the wherewithal to chase a definitive answer to where the fuck they were going.

"Willow, slow down. Cops crawl all over this side of town." Mostly due to the robberies and murders, but a rampant Bus chase wasn't outside the realm of possibility.

"It's good. They all know me."

He didn't know what that meant. Did she have a rap sheet? Oh, god. He would be lead story on the morning news: Chase Holbrook, power forward for the Pittsburgh Alloys, wanted in connection with a series of –what?—overnight.

"Willow, let me out. Like, here." He pointed to a street corner with a store advertising adult videos and peep shows.

She shot him a look like he had asked her to drive with her toes and sing show tunes. "I can't let you out here. This is not a safe neighborhood."

No shit. They were four blocks from his childhood turf. Sol's gym was as far south as he went. He hadn't been over here in a decade.

"Then why are we here?"

"This is where we make the most impact." She slowed down and pulled into an alley. "Keep your window up. Sometimes they get grabby."

And yet, she reached for the driver's side window crank.

"Grabby?" Strangled from his throat, the word sounded like the bad end of a prostate exam. His stomach went from mildly cramped to sliced and diced. Chase wondered if the code of chivalrous protection extended to crazy women who asked for crime. He checked the door lock. Twice.

"Yeah. They're just excited. Ready?" She held her hand out to him in expectation.

"For…?"

"You didn't think I was taking the nacho cheese to rub all over my body, did you?"

He had no words. But he realized she eyed the pack on his lap. He reached inside the bag, pulled out a cold, salted pretzel, and handed it to her.

An elderly black man hobbled up to her window.

"Hi, Grady. How are you feeling tonight?"

"Little hungry, Miss Bend."

"We can't have that." She motioned Chase for another pretzel and passed both out the window. "How's that hammer toe?"

"Better with them shoes you got me. Feel like I can dance again."

"Save a rhumba for me, will you?"

The man beamed. "Sure thing, Miss Bend."

Chase sank back into his seat. All the anger he harbored in his gut at the food in her stash dissipated on the cold wind spiraling through the vehicle. She was feeding the homeless. She was feeding the goddamned homeless, and it never occurred to him. Not once. Had he come so far from this existence that he didn't remember any of it?

She drove on, window still down, navigating the side street with care. When a grizzly guy in a Viking moustache and a dress approached her window, she reached her hand out and squeezed his.

"You're cold tonight, Sam. Did you try the church I mentioned?"

"They wouldn't let me in."

She reached for the hot dogs she had dropped beside her on the seat and handed him two. "Fill your stomach with this instead of liquor and there's nothing they won't do for you. You promised me. "

"I know."

"I don't want to see you here tomorrow. I want to know you went to Holy Cross. They've been expecting you. Handsomest guy in a dress in these parts."

"Yes, ma'am."

"Love you, Sam."

"Love you, too."

Chase's throat tightened at the genuine sentiment between them.

Willow drove on. "Sam got a Commendation Medal for valor in Vietnam. He came out to his children when he returned. They disowned him."

Next up was a woman named Millicent whose spine was so badly deteriorated, she looked only at the pavement. Willow told her how fancy she looked in her pink knit scarf—an item Chase strongly suspected Willow also had something to do with—and passed her a lipstick she had rolling around on her dashboard. "I thought this coral would go well with your beautiful skin color."

She turned to Chase and indicated a carton of French fries, adding in a whispered aside that Millicent had no teeth. This time, Chase wished Millicent a good night and waved, the first time he had spoken. He found the rush of the old woman's smile pretty damned close to the rush of a three-pointer.

He and Willow made a game of it—he anticipating a snack based on who came up to her car, always in motion, mostly a crawl, rarely stopping, and her telling an anecdote about each person. If she didn't know the person by name, she asked then introduced herself and Chase. Instead of using his real name, she introduced him as Magnum.

For once, he felt like someone who deserved that kind of name.

They drove the streets of his old neighborhood until the sack in his lap was empty and they had fed upwards of sixty people, many of them young, pregnant mothers or children. Chase stopped caring about his fatigue, his early morning shoot-around, the smells that permeated his clothes from the food and the air freshener. He hadn't had this much fun with his clothes on—outside of basketball—since that Bus trip with Marcus.

At one of the street corners, someone with a cell phone snapped a picture with a flash. It broke the spell. If someone snapped a photo, it would be all over the media, come tomorrow. Not that he had done anything wrong, but he had learned over the years that the mantra all press is good press just wasn't true. Give people something good and most manage to twist it into something sinister.

"I'd like to go back to my car now."

Willow seemed to sense it, too. For the first time that night, she was compliant and quiet. They sputtered and backfired all the way back to the arena. She navigated the Bus into the secured lot and stopped in front of his Hummer. The odd thought that one of his chrome wheels was probably worth more than the entire Bus crossed his mind. He became trapped in a surreal place between ringing her neck and thanking her for reminding him of all Sol had done to pull him out of his environment and show him he was worth something. He was reluctant to get out of the car. The cold. The fumes. Something.

"How long have you been doing that?"

"About three years."

"You do it every night?"

"Most home game nights. I petitioned the Alloy's GM and owner to have the leftover food the vendors would throw away at the end of the night. Told them it would be a great tax write-off and even better PR. They agreed."

"It's dangerous, Willow. I don't think it's a good idea."

"What do you know about danger? You have security around you 24-7."

He leveled a stare her direction. "More than you think. That neighborhood was mine once."

She puckered her lips, brow tight, as if she was assimilating this new information. When her expression eased, her nose tipped upward to the Bus's ripped roof as if she had exchanged food for haughtiness. "Kindness has no geographical boundaries."

"No, but crime has a definite zip code." He shook his head. There was no sense in reasoning with someone who defied reason at every turn. "Just be careful, okay? Might want to get a more reliable car."

"I'll get right on that once I've paid off the Learjet."

Once again, he felt like the asshole with the 90-million-dollar, four-year contract. He reached for the passenger door, trying to recall the charm that made it open.

"Is everything they say about you true?" Willow asked.

They. He couldn't begin to guess who—sports commentators, gossip rags, league players—or what—free agency mistakes, different woman every night, overpaid, undertalented, traitor to Sacramento. By the tone of her question, he knew something or someone had cast him in a negative light. Not that he cared what Bolt girl thought.

"What do you think?"

"I think Chase Holbrook, leading NBA scorer and playboy about town, wasn't the Chase Holbrook riding shotgun tonight."

Her edge had softened. Maybe he had offended her with his car comment. Maybe she had simply run out of her seemingly endless supply of energy. Or maybe, just maybe, he was growing on her a bit.

"And I believe Tarek," she added.

Uh-oh. Chase mentally braced himself. "What did he say?"

"That none of you are your image. And I should give you a chance."

He nodded. "That mean you'll be a bet monitor?"

"I'll think about it."

"Impulsive people aren't generally prone to thought."

"And thoughtful people aren't generally prone to impulses." The two of them in a nutshell. "Now get out. You're cramping my style. Being seen with you."

A laugh sputtered free of his lips. As expected, his door wouldn't open.

Willow scrambled in her seat so that her bare legs stretched across him and her ass wiggled up beside his hip, full-on childbirth position, no boundaries. He caught a whiff of the air freshener in her wake. She braced against the Bus's frame and pushed with her feet. The door popped open.

"John DeLorean?"

"John DeLorean." As if his name lent credence to her argument that the shit-brown Bus was a 'beaut.'"

He unfolded himself from the car, grabbed the duffel he had stashed at his feet, and turned in time to see her lean all the way across the seat, say "'Night, Magnum," and pull the door closed from the inside. She peeled out of the parking lot, her tailpipe erupting in gunfire at least twice on the way out of the parking lot.

Chase crawled into the plush interior of his SUV, locked his doors, and let the engine warm. He pulled out his cell phone, the text draft to Tarek just under his lock screen.

Rather live with your mother. Bet off.

He watched the blue cursor blink then hit the delete button. Delete, delete, delete, until the message was gone.

Estelle rose before *Good Morning, Pittsburgh*. Before the infomercials on television had switched over to regular programming, before electricity was no longer necessary to cut the darkness, before Willow had time to access REM sleep. Someone, somewhere along the way had convinced Estelle that walking her butt cheeks along the floor, legs extended, forward and backward, was good cardio for her heart. So every day at six a.m., Estelle squeezed her saggy bits into a leotard, à la Jane Fonda, and slayed the shag carpet in front of the couch like a greyhound with worms. When her labored exhales summoned the elderly gods of soft porn, Willow decided she'd had enough. She slipped on her coat and slippers, tiptoed out onto Estelle's back porch and called Dylan. She knew the hospital woke him up early.

His sleepy face appeared on her screen.

"Nice bed head," he said. "Where are you?"

She couldn't tell him she'd been evicted. No one in her family could know. News would spread like a contagion. She didn't need to give her parents any more ammunition for their argument that her life needed focus. Nor did she need any more offers of help, whether it was college tuition or connecting her to someone with a job that paid better than the Bolt gig.

"Outside."

"It's gotta be twenty degrees. I can see your breath."

She did her best to blow those fancy gangster-smoke rings. Didn't work.

"Say hi to Mike." Dylan turned the phone's camera lens to the hospital bed beside him. The two teen boys looked so out of place against walls painted with balloon-wielding pandas.

"Hi, Mike." Willow waved. When the camera angle returned to Dylan, she said, "I thought you had a private room."

"I gave it up. Some seven-year-old got banged up pretty bad in a traffic accident. Family never leaves his side. My old room had a couch with a fold-out bed. Besides, Mike here is the worst Super-Mario player in history. Makes me feel better about my scores."

Mike's protests rose above the video game noises.

Willow smiled. "They have you up early eating that oatmeal slop again?"

"Mike discovered the culinary art of Pop Rocks oatmeal."

"Party in your mouth."

"Exactly."

Willow knew Dylan's early mornings were filled with doctor's rounds, first round of PT for his prosthetic leg, and a host of blood tests to determine the progress of his osteosarcoma. Judging from the same bald head Mike sported, she guessed he was also there for cancer treatment.

"Hey, you think we can get Mike in to see Holbrook, too? He's a Knicks fan, but he said he'd put that aside for a chance to meet Chrissy La Roux."

At the mention of Chase, Willow's stomach fluttered awake. Kinda like that early-morning car sickness feeling after Denny's grand-slam hotcakes, but warmer. She had always kept it real with Dylan when the other adults in his life disappointed him and failed to treat him like the adult he almost was. But each conversation he mentioned meeting Chase, and each conversation she found a way to steer him in an entirely different direction. Previous night's excursion aside, Dylan deserved a real hero, not an as-played-on-the-court hero.

"Best aunt ever," Dylan said to Mike. "Courtside seats, the works."

"Just need a green light from your docs to travel." A green light she worried may never come.

"Hey, Dad's here. Want to say hi so I can put Mike away, once and for all?"

Willow's chest tightened. That her brother, Thomas, was at the hospital pre-dawn wasn't a good sign.

She kept her mood light. "Sure. Love you, Dyl."

"Love you, too, Wil. Say hi to Holbrook for me. Here's Dad."

Thomas commandeered the phone. The background streaked by, from the dimness of Dylan's room to a blinding, clinical light, Thomas clearly relocating to the privacy of the hallway. He wore his clean airline mechanic uniform and a somber expression.

"What's wrong, Thomas?"

"His levels have taken a turn, Wil. The pump isn't doing what they hoped."

The sub-freezing morning breeched her sheepskin-lined parka. She curled her knees to her chin and tried not to think of a world without Dylan's light.

"Does he know?"

"Not yet. But it's been one setback after another lately. He could really use something positive right now."

Willow knew what Dylan wanted that something to be.

"Did you talk to his doctor about travel?"

"He says there's restrictions on it. If it was some kind of Make-a-Wish, they'd have the funds for a nursing staff to travel with us to Pittsburgh, but we can't afford that."

At the mention of Make-A-Wish, tears sprouted. Dylan had been granted a wish. He had given it to an Army kid so she could see her father one last time at a meet-up in Germany. Another wish was in the works. But these things took time, and time was something none of them were sure Dylan had much of.

Willow thought about Chase's offer. *Hold up your end, it's all yours.*

She swiped at the snot freezing in her nose. "I'll see what I can do, Thomas."

"Wil?"

"Yeah?"

"Hurry, okay?"

She nodded, unable to speak, blew him a kiss, and ended the call. For another twenty minutes, she listened to the noises of the awakening city and watched night lift its hold over the skies. A plucky but faint Hank William's, Jr., song two-stepped out through the crack in the sliding glass door.

Dylan was such an amazing kid, so generous of spirit, so optimistic about the world, despite being dealt the shitty hand of cancer. If rumors about Chase were true—he only moved to the Alloys for the money, he was a man who only looked out for number one—he could crush everything that made Dylan, Dylan. And Willow refused to allow that on her watch. But on the off chance she learned the rumors weren't true, that knowledge would surpass any amount of money.

Even ten grand.

Willow went inside to pack.

5

Bzzz. Bzzzzz-bzz-bzzzzz.

"Coming. Jesus," Chase snapped as he stumbled out into his foyer, a sock dangling from his toes and tripping up his progress toward the relentless visitor. His pink boxers, imprinted with iced and sprinkled donuts, offered little protection against the morning chill. Reaching the door and pummeling whoever was assaulting his door chime had taken higher priority than finding clothes. He glanced through the peephole.

And saw the inside of a mouth.

Only one person he knew could be that on at seven in the morning.

"Willow." Her name slipped out like a muttered curse on his pasty tongue. He hunched in the chill, his hands cupping his junk as if she had the superpower of x-ray vision. "I'm sleeping."

"With your lips to the door? Sounds comfortable."

"I have a cold." He gave a sniff, just to sound convincing.

"I haven't been sick in five years. Killer immune system."

He was running out of viable excuses; he went for the jugular.

"I'm naked."

The shuffling on the other side of the door stopped. Dead silence.

Chase glanced through the peephole.

Willow stood blindfolded, her neck scarf pulled up over her eyes. It was the first time in recent memory a woman didn't jump at the chance to see him in his altogether. He found it refreshing.

He tapped his security code on the panel—surprising, because he barely remembered his own name this early—and opened the door.

She stood in a nest of suitcases and baskets and random crap that should have been boxed. Enough stuff to camp for weeks, months.

"You know I'm going to break the record soon, right?"

"I need all this to function."

"As a hoarder?"

He picked up a ceramic ethnic mask that was, quite possibly, the most disturbing thing he'd ever seen.

"As a woman of the world." She moved forward, hands extended, blindfold slipping. First, she ran into the door jamb and drew back as if she had touched a live wire. Then the wall of his chest—which she most certainly took her time inspecting.

Chase rolled his eyes, over the theatrics, and yanked down the holey scarf. Just as he suspected, the scarf was as thin as mosquito netting. He shoved the mask into her hands and walked back into his penthouse. "Not this world."

"Quetz here is a Central American god of wind or corn or something. Anyway, legend says he was tricked into drunkenness and sex with a celibate priestess."

Chase aimed for the refrigerator to put distance between his tired brain and the absurdity of letting this girl into his life, but she was hot on his tail, dragging her stuff along with the rest of the story.

"When he found out the priestess was his sister, he burned himself to death, and his still-beating heart became the morning star."

"Thank you for inhabiting my nightmares for the next decade." He poured a glass of orange juice and offered it to her.

"No thanks. I thought you could use some inspiration. To stay celibate."

"Lest I sleep with my sister and commit suicide by fire?"

"Okay, you know what? The lady at the bazaar hadn't had a sale all morning."

"Do you have an off switch?"

"No."

Chase took a swig of the semi-sour juice, thinking nothing would unscramble his mind but coffee, when he realized she was inspecting his underwear. He stepped closer to the counter for cover.

"Nice underoos. Don't see many men who can successfully pull off a Danish pattern near the netherod." She made a motion with her hands, a cross between a flourish and an air trombone, and capped it off with a two-note whistle. "Might want to steer clear of the windows in those. Last I saw, the traffic copter had shots of women on the roof next door holding binoculars."

"What?" Chase grabbed a hoodie from the back of a chair and shrugged it on then fumbled with the zipper before getting it to catch.

"There's also a swarm of scantily-clad women in the lobby, over-whelming Faustino. Don't you watch the news?"

Chase was so lost, he needed a miner's helmet and written directions. What did his doorman have to do with anything?

Willow grabbed the nearby television remote and switched on *Good Morning, Pittsburgh*. Next to a cartoon sun, the caption "Chase Holbrook's Shot at Love" lit the bottom third of the screen. She dialed up the volume.

The day's hard-hitting stories had already been exhausted. By the program's second hour, the network rolled out a panel of local socialites to give their take on all things irrelevant: winter color combinations, red carpet fashion critiques, Hollywood spats, and root jobs—whatever the hell those were.

"Women all over the city are waking up to the news that Alloys player and one of the most eligible bachelors in Pittsburgh, Chase Holbrook, has been overheard saying that he just can't meet the right girl but that he's ready to settle down with that special someone," said the Barbie-esque anchor. Chase remembered her giving him a full-court press at a kids' charity event last year.

"I never said that."

"Holbrook is quoted as saying that he doesn't have a type and so long as the woman has a kind heart, he's open to dating women of all shapes and sizes and backgrounds."

The burgeoning headache he had labelled Willow a few minutes earlier swelled to a migraine named Tarek. This stunt had Tarek all over it.

"As you can imagine," continued the anchor, "single women from all over the city are rising to the challenge. Literally."

The screen filled with the shaky live image of a group of women on a terrace, holding up signs with various enticements: CALL ME; Biggest Fan; I love your donuts!

"Oh, shit."

"At least you'll be smothered by women with kind hearts," offered Willow.

"Close the blinds." His voice was more hunted rabbit than suave pro-athlete.

"I didn't hear the magic word, Magnum."

Chase picked up Quetz. "Now, or your Mexican corn god bites it."

Willow grinned. "I have a better idea. Let's get them out of your face completely. C'mere." She went to the sliding patio doors and stood so that the terrace women would see her profile. Then she gestured at Chase.

He seethed for a moment then joined her, standing face to face. "What are we doing?"

"Showing them you've found your special someone. Down on one knee, champ."

"No. Trading this for rumors of my engagement is not a good swap. Every one of those women has a cell phone and is busy taking pictures and shooting video."

"I guess you're right." She curled her fingers in a come-here gesture. "Bend down, then."

He did, and she popped up onto her toes and whispered in his ear. "You've gotta admit I'm special, though."

Her scent—soap and cold air and cinnamon—wafted into his awareness, and he sucked in a breath. Her cheek brushed his as she sank back, and he couldn't help imagining what her lips would feel like in places other than his ear. Would she be skilled with her mouth in ways other than firing off sass and mockery? He suppressed a shiver and stepped back.

Willow had turned her attention to the women across the way. Their signs had lowered, and they had stopped jumping up and down. One or two were leaving. "Good enough." She looked from side to side. "There aren't any cords for the shades."

"There's a panel on the wall by the fireplace."

"Fancy."

He could have sworn she was taking her sweet-assed time. She pressed a button for the ceiling fan, the stereo—which thumped out a rousing dubstep before silencing—the spotlight over his Adolph Rupp trophy, again with the fan, then finally the blinds. Cloth shades closed on a barely-audible hum, meeting at the center and plunging the thirti-eth-floor space into nighttime.

"Fancy," Willow repeated. She padded back to the kitchen, turned off the television, and opened the fridge. "Got any empty jars?"

The woman whiplashed him with her topic changes. "Recycling bin." He pointed.

She fished out an empty mayo jar and washed and dried it at the sink; Chase could have collected an entire swarm of flies in his slack mouth.

"I'm afraid to ask."

"Got a black pen?"

"Far drawer by the coffee maker."

She uncapped the pen with her teeth and wrote L-U-S-T over the iconic yellow and blue label.

"What the hell is that?"

"It's like a swear jar, only for each impure thought, it's one dollar—the sum of which shall be given to charity at the end of my duties here." She placed the jar in a prominent place at the center of his kitchen table, adjusted it as if it were gem-encrusted and required a light beam of just the right angle to shine, and turned to pick up her suitcases. "Room?"

"Hallway by the fireplace. Third door on the left."

In passing, she scooped up Quetz and placed him shotgun in her armpit. "Might want to take the service elevator on your way to practice. There's enough skin in the lobby to fill the jar. Twice."

Chase buried his head in his hands and tried to massage away the tension building at his temples. He had just invited a circus into the most important stretch of games in his career. And he already owed the lust jar money.

Home game versus Charlotte. Sluggish start.

At the sixty-second gap between first and second quarter, Chase made his way to the team huddle. He knew Coach wouldn't send him in yet; his heart rate had yet to ease from seven straight minutes of humping up and down the wood. His attention drifted.

At center court, Bolt had dragged a young boy with some crazy dance moves out on the Alloy's logo. They traded move for move until the skit whipped the arena into cheers each time the little boy took his turn. After the boy's wickedly adorable Smooth Criminal dance move —hat and all—Bolt payed homage to him with a grand display of on-the-knees bowing.

Tarek shoved his shoulder.

Chase's focus snapped back to the huddle and ten sets of eyes on him —not the least of which was Coach Perkins, his stare expectant, as if he had just asked him a question whose answer would pivot the entire offensive push for the second quarter.

"Sorry, Coach."

"Holbrook is too busy checking out the mascot to tell us our mismatch. We turned over the ball six times in the last three minutes. You got to communicate and pay attention." Perkins fired those last words like an arrow between Chase's eyes. "I can't do it all from here."

He gave a surrender gesture with his clipboard and walked away. At the break in the huddle, a handful of rookies glanced at Chase as if he had just committed the crime of the century. Coach called a line-up change. Five fresh guys took the court.

Chase dropped into the padded, courtside chair. His blood ran toxic. How in God's name had he allowed Willow to hijack his focus?

Tarek dropped beside him.

"Man, you already hurtin' if you're looking at a blue muskrat like that."

Chase hadn't yet had a chance to confront Tarek for the morning prank. When they hadn't been part of team-orchestrated warm ups, Chase had ticked the time alone on the practice court. And when the game's announcer commented on the uptick in female fans at the game and asked for a shout-out from the ladies only—deafening in pitch and intensity—Chase had avoided eye contact with Tarek. He had been waiting until after the game, but Tarek's smart-ass smile nearly put Chase over the edge.

Tarek's mother would find the fake positive pregnancy test Chase planted soon enough.

6

Chase's Hummer carved fresh ruts into the snow outside the arena. He had wasted a good half hour searching for Willow—not because he particularly wanted to find her, but because it was as important as ever to win the bet against Tarek after his morning stunt. Part of Chase felt a slight tug toward the prospect of delivering left-over vendor food to the south side. Most of him just wanted his terrace hot tub and his favorite barbeque take-out.

Willow, however, was not on the court or in the laundry room. No one had seen her, and she wasn't answering her cell.

He decided she had taken advantage of the extra key he had left on the island. As off-kilter as she was, he trusted her. She was a steward of so many, putting others first at every turn. He just hoped she extended that same courtesy with his possessions.

Flurries blew in circular eddies against his windshield. His wipers swiped away the accumulation, lighter now than the measurable amount squeaking beneath his tires. He drove past the robotic arm of the secured lot and glanced out at the sea of white.

And the lone hump of a car, dusted in snow, with its hood raised.

Chase squinted through the flakes. From the angle of the car, he could tell someone was buried beneath the hood. He slowed to a crawl while he contemplated his next move. Best case: he helps someone out. Worst case: he gets robbed at gunpoint.

Even worse case: it was Willow.

Everything with her was ten times more involved than he bargained for. The woman didn't know the definition of simple. But stranger, criminal, or Willow, he knew he couldn't enjoy his brisket with special sauce until he offered to help.

He navigated his SUV closer. A parking lot lamp cast an eerie orange glow on the distressed vehicle and something blue. Closer, he saw the furry rump of a costume wiggle under the hood.

Chase braked and shifted into park. He tipped his head back against the headrest and sighed. Willow wouldn't do a simple lift back to his place and call for roadside. His stomach growled, one final plead before it kissed a warm, spicy, post-game dinner goodbye.

The Hummer's high headlights illuminated the area beneath the Bus's engine compartment. Neck up and one costume-free naked arm, she was Willow in pigtails. Neck down, she was a blue muskrat turned abominable snow monster. Her free right hand worked something inside the van.

He popped out of his toasty vehicle. Before he had a chance to ask her the problem, she straightened and fired off a question only Willow could have at that moment.

"Got any pantyhose?"

Chase patted his ass and thighs and reloaded his voice with heavy sarcasm. "Damn. I left my control-top fishnets in the locker room."

"Cute." She flashed him a patronizing smile. "None of your super-model dates left any in the back of that overpriced tank?"

"You're hardly in a position to be casting stones at my ride." He ducked his head under the hood, mostly to block the icy north wind. He knew shit about broken-down cars. Less than shit. "What's the problem?"

"Broken belt. If I had pantyhose I could wrap it around the pulleys and tie it off."

"How do you know so much about cars?"

"I dated a grease monkey once. How do you know so much about pantyhose?"

"I dated a Lakers girl once."

She rolled her eyes, this time accompanied by a half-grin. His gaze trailed to her bare arm, so strangely out of place in this setting, in this cold. So completely fit, the slight contours cast shadows.

"Come on. I'll give you a ride."

"No thanks. I'll find other wheels. I'm not going back to your place, anyway."

This news did not hit him as he'd expected. He had been waiting to hear her say those words since this absurd bet began. Now that she had uttered them, his lungs took in less frigid air and his body tinged with an odd vacancy.

"You're not?" Crap. His question came out anything but unaffected.

"Nope."

"Let me guess—another of your Girl Scout missions?"

"Girl Scouts kicked me out. I was too…"

"Wild?"

"Unconventional. I gave away all my cookies."

His laugh came out on a cloud-burst. "Doesn't surprise me."

"I do have a visit to make. You up for it?"

"Will there be food? I'm starving."

"I can get you mashed potatoes. That's all I can promise. And not even very good ones."

"Tempting."

"I can't disappoint, Chase. People are depending on me."

Her tone had sobered, left him behind—again. She attacked this philanthropy thing like he attacked basketball. One look past her flake-covered lashes to the hope beyond, and he couldn't say no.

"Mashed potatoes it is."

Willow squealed and bounced and filled his arms with a fifty-pound, damp muskrat pelt and one semi-warm arm slinked around his bare neck before she caught herself. The unexpected touch skipped heat down his spine and awakened his frozen sub-waist parts, groin to toes. He dismissed the sensation as the rush that came from helping someone else. Deep down, he knew that rush wouldn't have come from helping just anyone. Helping someone who did nothing but help others carried a special weight.

They secured the Bus and climbed into his SUV. The smell of sweaty, damp balls eclipsed the new leather of his current-model-year Hummer. Bolt's head filled his backseat, glaring at him in the rear view mirror with psycho eyes. Somehow, he didn't care. Clearly, the mascot was part of the mission.

"Where to?"

"Pearson Children's Hospital."

Chase glanced at his dash readout: 11:58. "This time of night?"

"Always."

At the emergency room doors to the hospital, the only entrance open this late, Willow placed Bolt's head on her shoulders and turned to Chase. She didn't know why she cared what he thought, but she asked anyway.

"How do I look?"

"Hideous."

She marched through the emergency wing, waving at staff members on her way to the elevators. Willow took the vow of mascot silence very seriously.

Well, mostly. "What do you have against Bolt?"

"Nothing personal, really. I don't like any mascots."

They reached the deserted lobby, and she punched the up arrow.

"That's un-sportsmanlike, un-fandom, un-American," she said.

"Too much like clowns. I don't like them, either."

Bolt's head sweltered from her labored exhales. Sweat squeezed from her pores. "That's just wrong. Clowns get a bad rap. Their sole purpose is bringing joy. The world could use a little more of that."

"I don't disagree. I just don't need mascots and clowns bringing joy into my world."

Chase was so closed-minded, so elite, he couldn't even access that part of his soul that housed innocent fun. When he wasn't chasing the net in search of glory, his world was plastered all over the nightly entertainment shows with photos of L.A. beach parties and French

Riviera yachts. Every time his diamond-encrusted fortress crumbled a bit, she was reminded why he was the worst role model for Dylan.

"Right. You have Hollywood actresses for that."

"You say that like they're all snakes. They're good people. Most of them. You don't have the market cornered on kindness, you know." Though his words were muffled through the mutant-sized mask on her head, his tone contained enough armor to forge the Rutgers Scarlet Knight costume.

Since she couldn't fire back what she really wanted to say—how absurd the notion that she somehow did any of this to gratify some self-stroking agenda—she reared back, Bolt's paw fanned to his muskrat nose, and wiggled her hairy digits.

"Nice. Very mature."

Was that why he was here? To stroke his ego? She had a plan for that. His ego couldn't be stroked if no one knew he was there. Maybe this outing would help him see the good he could do, help him see the world beyond his gilded existence.

They entered an open elevator and rode up to the third floor in silence. Willow planned to seek out Loretta first. She was the RN on night duty this week who had called Willow to let her know Javier had asked about Bolt. He was a ten-year-old who wanted to be the first Latino American president. Javier could name all forty-three U.S. presidents and their vice-presidents sworn into office—Grover Cleveland being the notable exception that had messed with the consecutive numbers—and one little-known fact about each one. Her personal favorite was Herbert Hoover, who donated his entire executive office salary to charity. Javier also had end-stage leukemia.

Loretta lit up when she saw Bolt coming. Or maybe it was Chase standing beside her. Willow had never heard the woman so tongue-tied in her greeting.

Willow pointed at Javier's room.

"Up watching a rerun of the game, as usual."

More hospital staff gathered. For midnight, the floor sure was hopping. Then Willow noticed they were all women. She grabbed Chase's hand and dragged him into a snack room for families and visitors. The door suctioned closed behind them.

She lifted off Bolt's head.

"What?"

"You never asked me why I visit here at night."

"Why do you visit here at night?"

"Because at this time of day, it's all about the kids. There aren't parents around wanting me to pose for photos with healthy siblings or hospital PR execs pulling me away from the patients. It's just a few staff members and the kids here who need the kind of happiness Bolt brings."

"So…?"

"So you being here in all your blazing hot…Gordon Ramsay glory has unearthed every female staff member in this wing of the hospital."

Chase laughed, a show of impeccable teeth and lips that would have caused mass cardiac arrest had they been in the hallway. "Gordon Ramsay does it for you, huh?"

"He's passionate and…" She squeezed her eyes closed, her frustration bubbling to the surface. "Totally irrelevant to my point."

"What do you want me to do, hide?"

"Better. You'll be Bolt tonight."

"No." His no was so swift, she knew he hadn't considered the beauty of being inside a costume, sweaty ball smell or not.

"Wearing a costume means you don't have to pretend to be anyone else. No expectations of how Chase Holbrook, power forward for the Pittsburgh Alloys, would behave."

"I'm six-foot-eight, Willow."

"There's plenty of room in here. Bolt just won't be so…saggy."

"You're forgetting my strong dislike of mascots."

"You shouldn't knock something until you've tried it. Afterward, if you still dislike mascots, I will respect your opinion on the matter because it comes from a place of authority."

"I don't know…" He did that thing he often did where he scrubbed his face with his palm, eyes pleading toward the ceiling.

"There's a boy out there in room 3042 who wants a blue muskrat all to himself. Don't make him share Bolt with twenty horny nurses."

God's truth, Chase blushed. Magnum underwear man blushed. It was glorious.

"One kid. If I hate it, we swap back."

Willow crossed her fuzzy heart with Bolt's paw.

"All right."

She rocked out a jazzy dance move and wiggled out of the costume, firefighter-style. All Chase had to do was step inside.

Except Chase didn't move.

She followed his stare, thinking she had been outed with massive sweat stains or something, but all she saw was her usual under-Bolt clothes—a sports bra and boy shorts. "What?"

If he had blushed before, he was certifiably apple-colored now—hairline to neck. She realized what had him so freaked and turned so her back was to him.

"I won't look."

"I'm not stripping."

"You'll bake."

"It's snowing outside."

"And it's Phoenix in July inside Bolt. Besides, I need something to cover."

He released a dramatic sigh like a teenaged girl deprived of her cell phone and seeing her crush, all on the same day. She really thought she had the whole Chase Holbrook-nearly-naked thing down, but the sound of his warm-up pants unfastening—snap, snap-snap—had his late-night commercial flashing through her brain. She couldn't become another one of those simpering females who basked in his nearness. Even if he had Gordon Ramsay beat. By a mile—or kilometer, depending on the continent. She was the one keeping him on the straight and narrow. Tarek trusted her character.

His jacket and pants draped her shoulder. With them came his freshly-showered scent—clean and sophisticated and far richer than the Irish Spring that always occupied Estelle's shower because she had once fallen in love with a married Irishman. Willow focused on snack-sized chocolate cookies in the vending machine because it kept her from worrying about her own stench after occupying the costume all evening, and it kept her mind off of a treat of a very different variety. And because, well, chocolate.

The unmistakable zzzzrup of the closure at Bolt's side seam was her cue to turn. She took in the muskrat body and the GQ head.

And laughed. Classic. Like one of those flip games for kids.

"I'm done." He reached near his neck to unzip.

"Don't. I'm sorry." She brought her hand down over his. Her touch lingered far longer than she intended, which made everything in that room as awkward as if she'd had sweat stains from the get-go. He broke the tension first.

"I was wrong."

"About what?"

"It isn't sweaty balls. It's Nunzio's feet."

Willow giggled. "Lean forward."

Chase complied. She dropped Bolt's head over Chase's with an unceremonious plop.

"You look amazing. Get ready to make someone's day."

"I can't see in this thing." His voice was muffled but amused.

"Bolt doesn't talk."

She slipped on his jacket, still warm from his body, then gathered his paw and led him out into the hallway. Women in scrubs gave them strange looks then went about their business.

"What do I do?" he whispered.

"Just be you."

7

———

Willow and Chase-dressed-as-blue-muskrat entered Javier's room. The little boy's eyes widened when he looked past her at his other more exotic guest.

"Bolt!"

Had Javier not been tethered by IVs and medicine drips, he would have ambushed the mascot. Bolt drew close to the bed and gave an awkward wave.

So it wasn't Broadway, but it did take some practice to get into character.

Javier waved back then hugged Willow. He wore a blue Alloys jersey with Tarek's number on it and pajama bottoms patterned with basketballs.

"Hi, Wil."

"Hey, champ. Looking good. You're wearing my favorite player's jersey."

Bolt went all paws-on-hips. She imagined Chase's expression in contrast to Bolt's open-mouth OOOOh face.

"Dad says they were sold out of Holbrook ones. He has one on backorder."

At this newsy tidbit, Bolt did a triumphant victory squirm complete with we-are-the-champion fist pumps. This sent Javier in to a fit of giggles, which, in turn, egged Bolt on to more moves.

Willow laughed. She swiped Javier's phone off the nightstand and captured a few choice moves so he could show the other kids in the cancer wing. Never in a million years would she have expected Chase Holbrook to floss and nae nae in a blue muskrat costume. She picked up Javier's bedside phone and dialed the hospital kitchen.

"Food services. Alex speaking."

"Hey, Alex, it's Willow."

"Finally decided to grace us with your presence, eh?" he teased.

"You know how busy the season gets," said Willow. "How's that cute little Malamute puppy of yours?"

"Chewing on everything."

"Text me pictures. I'm sure he's so much bigger now than when I last saw him."

Javier snagged her attention with a perfectly-executed dab. Bolt dabbed, too.

"Thanks for the vet recommendation. She's great. What can I send up tonight?"

"I promised mashed potatoes. A lot of them. And lime Jell-O."

"Got you covered, love."

"You're the best, Alex."

By the time she hung up with Alex, Javier had conned Bolt into sitting beside him in bed. The contrast in size was staggering. Javier looked a little like a flesh wound on the elbow of a blue muskrat. They watched the rerun of Chase juking a star Charlotte player and sailing past for an easy layup. To say Javier and Bolt celebrated was an understatement.

The final few minutes of the game played out. Javier reached for the remote and turned off the television. When Bolt tried to give him more room to settle back into bed, the boy grabbed Bolt's furry elbow and held him in place. Bolt stretched out again beside him.

Javier sighed. Contentment, fatigue from battling an illness most of his life, something. His beautiful nut-brown skin had a grayish cast. Willow planted herself at the foot of his hospital bed next to legs-for-days Bolt and dug deep for positivity to surpass her melancholy.

"Miss Loretta said you were riding a scooter up and down the hallway yesterday."

"Yep."

"Did you show 'em how it's done?"

Javier did a neck jive and swiped a suave hand past the place he once had an enviable mane of thick, dark hair.

Willow laughed. The kid had serious charm. Total ladies' man, if he ever got the chance to become a man at all.

"How's your mom?"

"Sad most days."

"She's afraid one of those cute blondes down the hall will become your girlfriend. Steal you away from her."

A fast grin played at Javier's mouth but subsided almost as quickly. "I think she knows."

"Knows what?"

"That I have to go soon."

Willow's throat thickened. She didn't know exactly what he meant, certainly didn't want to make a joke of it.

"Go where, Javier?"

"Heaven."

Willow's chest swelled, to bursting, almost painful. Instincts had her glancing at Chase, but all she saw was Bolt's silly expression.

"How do you know?"

"My grandpa comes most nights after Mom leaves. Sometimes he'll sit in that chair over there until I fall asleep, so I'm not scared. We talk."

"What do you talk about?"

"He tells me what heaven's like. He says it's different for everyone, but that joined souls stay together. Like a love gravity."

"Sounds amazing." Tears backed up. Willow fought—hard—to subvert them from her eyes, but they crackled out through her voice.

"I think so, too. I hope they have basketball there."

Bolt sat up slowly. He turned to face her, his hands resting at the base of the costume head.

Chase was asking permission. Willow nodded.

Chase removed Bolt's head. "I hope they have basketball, too."

Javier's eyes flashed cartoon-wide. His jaw dropped. Three-Stooges-like hand gestures followed. He glanced from Willow to Chase, Willow to Chase, mouth gaped.

"I'm glad I said your jersey was my first pick," said Javier.

Chase laughed. Somber moment aside, they worked at devising a bro-handshake, paw to small hand. When that didn't work, Chase unzipped Bolt's costume and freed his right hand. The handshake grew to epic proportions, something she could never remember, but Chase learned it with the finesse of someone who had memorized an entire NBA playbook.

A knock sounded at the door. Alex came in with a loaded tray—far more than mashed potatoes and Jell-O. He, too, failed to hide his surprise at seeing Chase there, but gave his utmost attention to Javier.

"Someone told me you might want a little midnight snack." He set the tray on the patient table and pressed the bed panel to elevate the mattress behind Javier's head.

"Three green Jell-Os?"

"All for you, my man."

"Thanks."

Chase introduced himself and shook Alex's hand. After a brief trifecta of male commentary on the Charlotte game, Alex said his goodbyes.

"I can't eat all this. Want some?" Javier asked Chase.

"I thought you'd never ask."

Together, they mowed through chili-cheese fries, steamed green beans, mashed potatoes, two cartons of chocolate milk and the fattest slice of lemon-meringue pie Willow had ever seen. Turns out, Javier wasn't only an expert on presidents. He was a bit of a basketball historian, which led to an endless and spirited debate about the true greats of the game. They took selfies, Chase still half in Bolt's costume. For once, the mascot code didn't matter. Not much did, except the possibility that Willow might have been wrong—very wrong—about Chase Holbrook.

It wasn't a big deal that Chase couldn't sleep. Today was a day off before a two-game road trip out to L.A. He could make up for being awake at four in the morning, watching muted highlights from around the NBA, by sleeping all day if he wanted. It wasn't even a big deal that he had veered off his strict diet, designed for peak season performance, and overindulged in the best-tasting, greasiest chili-cheese fries in recent memory. What was a big deal was the source of his sleeplessness.

Willow.

In the two years since he had joined the Alloys, he never once bothered to look past her pigtails and sassy mouth and irritating positivity. Knowing what he knew of her now, everything fit. The taunting in her act. The need to have someone high-energy like Willow fill a costume that represented the team and the game. Basketball made people like Chase and Javier happy, but a ton of people who came to games for other reasons craved that happiness, too. After filling her shoes, literally, in both costume and deed, he had a new appreciation for how much she gave. He hadn't seen that level of selflessness since Sol and Irma.

But where did it end?

He knew next to nothing about the woman sharing his place except who she was in the eyes of others. What did *she* want? No one aspired to be a team mascot. Her words from the hospital snack room returned to him. Wearing a costume means you don't have to pretend to be anyone else. Did that mean that when she wasn't Bolt, she was pretending?

From the kitchen, the hush of slippers on tile brought him clear of his thoughts. He peered over the leather back of his sofa and caught a glimpse of her sneaking a glass from his cabinet and filling it at the sink. He had an entire shelf in the fridge of imported spring water from the French Alps, and she went for tap water.

That wasn't all he noticed.

Willow wore the jersey Javier gave her earlier that night. Kid said he had a better one on the way, which damn near made Chase prouder than the day he'd learned about his offer for a contract from Pittsburgh.

She wore little else.

The hem and square NBA logo skimmed just shy of the swell of her ass and the ample arm holes promised a show from the side should she decide to reach for anything above her shoulders. He wanted to march into the kitchen and give her a reason to stretch for something on a high shelf. He felt like a creep, watching her without saying anything.

She chugged the water in an unabashed display of rampant thirst, set the glass on the counter, and said, "Now why can't your head be on a swivel like that on defense?"

Shit. Busted.

"Why do you give me such a hard time? More than any other player?"

An honest question. He wanted to know if Willow was one of the naysayers—the ones who believed the Alloys would have been stronger had they gone a different direction, the ones who believed he tied up funds for younger, healthier players straight out of the draft, the ones who counted the days until the Alloys were free to negotiate him gone. He knew she would shoot straight. No pandering to what he wanted to hear, like so many others.

Shh-shh-shh. Her slippers drew near until she stood before him. God help him, he couldn't keep his eyes off of her bare legs, unless he counted the snag when his gaze slid to her ankles and he marveled at the colossal unicorns that had swallowed her feet. His hands twitched from the desire to reach out and touch her, to skim his fingers up her leg to her ass and pull her close.

"Well, shirtless boy wonder, a long time ago, I learned that every time I gave you a hard time on the court, you got fired up enough to come back and do something remarkable. I started to believe that I might have a small part in that."

He wanted to tell her she didn't need him to be remarkable—that she already had remarkable covered simply by being her. She'd opened his awareness, he realized, beyond basketball. Beyond scoring, in both senses of the term. She wasn't the annoying mascot girl anymore.

"You do," he said, chagrined to admit it. "You do have a part in that. Willow…" He bit back an invitation to join him on the sofa. He had a hunch that would not be a good way to win his bet. There was too much emotion he didn't know what to do with. For him, all emotion was connected to the game. No attachments, no expectations. South side had taught him that.

She yawned and padded toward her hallway on a barely audible "Night." At the last minute, she veered to her purse by the door, dug through her wallet, and dropped a bill in the lust jar.

Chase waited until he heard her door click shut, then he added a ten of his own.

Symphony, an exclusive restaurant and pub with a view of the Los Angeles skyline, had a four-month waiting list. Unless your name was Chase Holbrook or Tarek Johns. Tarek had arranged a double date during the team's evening gap in the city—Tarek with his sister, who was a talent scout for an up-and-coming west coast agency, and Chase with one of her rising stars—a bit-part actress named Fallon whose greatest roles to date included a toothpaste commercial and a distressed assault victim on a crime drama. The ambiance was minimalistic and grayscale, in keeping with the theme of music for the taste buds. What Chase found most minimalistic, however, was his date. She had shiny, chocolate-brown hair, perfectly symmetrical features, a smile too perfect to be real, airbrushed makeup—total sabotage on Tarek's part. Gorgeous but wasteful.

She took three bites of her ethereal salmon—whatever the hell that was—and shooed it back on the waiter. Her next three courses were no exception. Chase mentally accumulated the discarded food and thought of Grady and Sam and Millicent.

"If you don't like the food, we can go somewhere else," he said to her.

"It isn't that. I have a callback for a beach series next week. They want me to run lines in a bikini."

He looked at Tarek, whose raised brows said a million things his mouth didn't. Chase gave a faint shake of his head and dug into his filet mignon.

At Tarek's sister's request, they had agreed to conversation that did not include basketball. This left out talk about Chase's highest scoring game yet—44 points. He attributed his recent hot streak to the celi-bet —not because he was completely sold on the premise but because Willow always had somewhere to be, someone to help. During those times, he put in hours alone on the practice court. Gave him time to think.

Mostly about her.

Chase glanced over at the gorgeous woman beside him. He tried to get lost in Fallon's full, ruby lips as she ate, but the collagen she had discussed with Tarek's sister earlier tainted his appreciation. He tried to find a glimmer in her caramel-colored eyes as she spoke about her days as a pageant contestant, but he detected no passion behind her words. He tried to imagine her flawless body grinding against him in some secluded place with an infinity pool and moonlight, but she became Willow.

Jesus Christ.

He excused himself from the table and went out on the empty patio for fresh air. It wasn't long before he heard Tarek's smug voice behind him.

"She's gettin' to you, isn't she?"

"You're an asshole, Johns." His voice had all the strength of a wet paper towel. Accompanied with a half-smile, insults were just something they did. "I'm not losing this bet."

"Who said this had anything to do with the bet?" Spoken like a choirboy hiding a skin mag behind his back.

"C'mon, man. Look at her. Her toes have been humping my shin all night."

Tarek clapped his hands. "Priceless."

"I want to go back to the hotel."

"Now you're talkin'."

"Alone."

"Man, are you feverish?" He reached for Chase's forehead.

Chase smacked it away.

"You know how many men on this earth have a chance with Fallon Grey? Hell, I don't even have a chance with Fallon Grey, and I'm the best-looking cat on the team."

"I'm perfectly capable of making conversation about things other than basketball, but she hasn't stopped talking all night. About stupid shit. Like butt glue so she doesn't get a wedgie during her audition. Is that supposed to turn me on?"

"For your wallet's sake, let's hope not."

Chase stared at the intersection of a nearby palm tree and the warm L.A. skyline at dusk. So unlike Pittsburgh. What if the sports broadcasters were right? Should he have stayed in Sacramento? In this state, the fans loved him unconditionally. At least they did before he bailed—back when he was fresh out of the draft, loyalty intact. Was Willow right? Had his joy come from chasing money and notoriety? Did that make him as shallow as Fallon Grey?

Tarek sidled up to the railing beside him, the jokester in him all but leeched out. "We're celebratin', man. You played like Jordan out there today. No one could touch you. You're about to beat my ass in the record books. Food's good. Place is chill. So we go back and start up a conversation about something else. Anything else. You name it. Just don't tap out on me, or I'm left with my sister all night."

Chase thought about his medium-rare steak. Goddamned perfection that shouldn't go to waste. Tarek was right. They were celebrating. Chase had worked his ass off to get to his level—sleeping, breathing, and eating the game until it consumed him. He'd be damned if he'd let a space-ace woman three-thousand miles away get in his head and ruin his night.

8

Chase returned to the table at Symphony, a slight shift in his frame of mind and spirits improved. They cleared their plates. Wine flowed for the ladies. Fallon nudged his cock under the tablecloth, the promise of so much more in her pointed stare. He could call a cab and have her six ways until morning, infinity pool and moonlight and whatever else he could think of to bankroll.

The four companions spilled out onto the downtown street below.

Chase glanced across the street. A man in filthy clothes and bare feet sat against the bank tower, holding a cardboard sign.

The sight immobilized him. His culinary feast turned to an anchor in his gut.

Tarek called out to him, the back of a cab propped open, ladies already inside. "Come on, man."

Chase's stare again drifted across the street. A couple walking by gave the man a wide berth.

"Hold up. I'll just be a minute."

Chase jogged across six lanes, mostly empty. Tarek's words filled the space behind him, a best-friend blend of curses, questions, and white guy slams. He stood apart from the seated man, easily in his sixties, by a good ten feet. For the first time, hairs rose on his neck. What if this guy pulled a knife on him? Then he read the sign.

Too damned ugly to prostitute. Hungry and tired.

Chase suppressed a smile. This guy was all right. Honest. Like someone else Chase knew.

He tried to think what Willow would say. With her, it was never about someone's misfortune. Always, she made it about their shared humanity. And without fail, she made sure someone on this earth knew their name.

"I'm Chase."

"What do you chase?" The man raised his head.

"Women, mostly. Balls, sometimes."

"Hopefully it's not women with balls. Seen a few of those in my day."

Chase gave an appreciative laugh. Already the guy was more entertaining than Fallon.

"What's your name?"

"They call me Crazy Jack."

"What did your mom call you?"

"Worthless, mostly. But on Sundays, she called me Clarence."

Chase drew close and held out his hand. "Nice to meet you, Clarence. Mind if I sit?"

Clarence completed the handshake. "Free country. Least that's what they told me when I enlisted."

Chase settled beside him, his back to the building. This gave him a prime view of Tarek pacing and two bobbing heads inside the shadowy cab craning, watching.

"Thank you for your service, Clarence."

Clarence just rattled a wiry exhale through the maze of overgrowth in his nostrils, past his grizzled beard.

"I was hoping you could give me some advice." Since meeting Willow, honesty felt like a drug. A safe, league-sanctioned hit of something refreshing and real.

"Shoot."

"There's this woman…"

"Always."

A slight grin tugged at Chase's lips. "She's impossible. In-your-face. Opinionated. Not even particularly gorgeous, but kind of cute in a girl-next-door way. Adorable, really, when she isn't completely frustrating me."

"So what's the problem?"

"I have to be guarded. People tend to come into my life for the wrong reasons."

"And you think she's one of them?"

"Everyone before her has put conditions on me." If you get all-state, Chase. Top-tier, Chase. First round, Chase. Then we'll talk. Then we'll see. "It's hard to believe any different."

"Sounds like a lonely life."

His brain catalogued the women, the college friends, the parasites who wanted to share his limelight. "Sometimes."

"Sure you're not using them, too?"

Chase glanced across the road at Tarek. His hands were open, spread wide, all "What the hell?" Maybe life was one big game, everyone using everyone else in some way to get ahead. Hadn't he done the same to dig himself out of the slums? Hustling pick-up games to eat. Pitting guys against each other to drive competition. Sports agents, business managers, even teammates. Tarek setting up a night with a beautiful woman to win the bet. Maybe people like Willow were a myth, and she would show her colors soon enough.

"Doesn't matter. I don't need her kind of distraction. I have something important to do."

"Something more important than the affections of a woman?"

"Yes."

"Then I'd say you're the one with the problem, bub."

"She would like you, Clarence."

"Sounds like a keeper to me."

A ripple of warmth stirred where his anxiety had been. He let loose a laugh and slipped off his dress shoes.

"They're not very practical. Hurt my feet, actually. I'm used to different footwear. Mind if I leave them?"

Clarence shrugged. "Suit yourself."

"Thanks for the wisdom, Clarence."

Chase reached for his hand again. This time, Clarence's grip had the strength of a solid connection. On his way to standing, Chase slipped two crisp bills out of the money clip in his pocket and buried them inside the right shoe.

"Sure thing, ball-chaser."

He couldn't be sure if Clarence recognized him. Something in the way the old man said it suggested he did. Chase dodged a bit of traffic on his way back to the cab.

Tarek pointed at Chase's stockinged feet as they climbed into the van. "Those were Ferragamos."

Fallon looked at him with a warped expression. A little like she had put butt glue between her perfectly-painted eyebrows. A little like he was a few buckets short of a win.

"Insane, man," muttered Tarek.

Chase smiled. He had never felt saner.

Hands down, Willow's Aunt Nonnie's New Orleans gumbo was the best on the planet. She had spent the morning shopping at the freshest markets, making seafood stock, shucking oysters and peeling shrimp, steaming crab claws, and chopping veggies. The spicy scents filling Chase's never-been-touched, chef-inspired kitchen were to die for. Add the buttermilk cornbread she had baked that morning, and the spread was fit for a Cajun king.

Or, at least, the entire lineup of Alloys players.

Early that morning, she had heard Chase come home after the team's red-eye flight back from the west coast. Willow stayed in bed. Mostly, she kept herself from sleeping by wondering random things. Why was she planning a huge dinner when she should be looking for an apartment? Had Chase christened every bed in the penthouse? Did Gordon Ramsay drop F-bombs during sex like he did when cooking? When was Estelle's prescription ready for pick up? Was there a television hidden in her room like in every other room in this penthouse? What if it was on the ceiling and had a camera and…Crap! Her thoughts had diverged into sweaty, brazen Chase-sex until she'd buried her head under a pillow as punishment.

Willow caught a shower before the team showed up. She chose a shirt Nonnie had sent her with a waving cartoon crayfish that read "Laws, yeah. I'm cray," and wrapped a red apron around the waist of her yoga pants, sous chef-style. By six, the place was hopping with towering men whose visual feast rivaled her edible one.

"So this is where the Gordon Ramsay preoccupation comes from. You cook." Chase entered the kitchen, snagged a pinch of cornbread from the platter, and popped it into his mouth.

Scratch that. Something else rivaled the cayenne-hot visual feast dotting the penthouse: Chase Holbrook's orgasmic eye roll at her culinary skills.

"That's really good," he said around the crumbly bite. "If your gumbo is anything like your cornbread, you should open a place."

She stared into the biggest gumbo pot and bit her lip. Should she tell him? To her parents, her idea had been one crumb on a rabbit trail through Indecisive Forest. Just another of Willow's hare-brained ideas to keep from focusing on nursing school or any one thing that might give her a stable life. It had been her dream. All hers. And that held power she didn't give away lightly.

"Actually…I've been thinking about it."

"Yeah?"

"I want to open a pay-it-forward restaurant."

"What's that?"

"Okay, picture this…" She set her wooden spoon across the pot's lip and hopped up on the counter, jazzed that he asked. "It opens somewhere between the trendy part of downtown and the neighborhood we drove through. There are no menu prices and every person who orders receives a check for zero dollars. They can pay for their meal by volunteering—working the organic garden on the roof, serving others, cooking, dishwashing—or they can pay for the next person or two or twenty who comes through the door. The walls are filled with messages of encouragement, left behind by those who have come before. I want to call it The Cordial Café…or something like that."

She braced herself for comments she had heard before. From her father: Is that a sustainable business? From her mother: Oh, honey, it sounds nice, but what about being a nurse? From her brothers: Let us know when you wake up in the real world. From Estelle: What if one of the volunteers blows his nose in the food? Health department fiasco. Willow braced herself for Chase to fall into the same comfortable, teasing territory they had established regarding the Bus, but he flashed his devastatingly handsome but contradictory one-two combo of a head shake and a smile.

"What?" she asked.

"Nothing. No, it's great."

"You're shaking your head."

"I've just never met anyone so passionate about helping others before."

He picked up the wooden spoon and stirred the gumbo in a neighboring pot, right where she'd left off. Maybe he needed a diversion. Maybe he just liked having a hand in things. The domesticity of the small act was a thousand times sexy.

She glanced around at his well-appointed kitchen, a stark contrast from the olive-green stoves and cracker-box workspaces of her life.

"Too bad it'll never happen." She sighed.

"Who says?"

"Everyone. I can't even figure out my own life. How will I ever run a business?"

"You know the food and the heart behind the idea. Get a partner who knows the restaurant industry and an investor or two."

"I'm trying to save up the money on my own. I don't want to be beholden to investors. They expect profits and crap like that."

He shot her a narrow-eyed glance but didn't say anything. He shook his head then turned back to the pot, tending it as if he expected the seafood to jump out and waddle back to the ocean. In profile, she saw his mouth twitch and flirt with his barely-there dimple.

"I heard you showed masterful control in the face of adversity on your date," she teased.

Tiny droplets along his hairline held her attention. Steam from the rolling boil or perspiration? No matter the cause, sweat was, quite possibly, his best color.

"I held my own."

"That's what Tarek said." She hopped off the counter and nudged him, shoulder to elbow. He had walked right into that innuendo, and she wouldn't let him squirm out of it for anything. "So…I called a tow truck for my car, and they said they couldn't find it in the arena lot."

The Bus had mysteriously shown up, alternator belt replaced, while Chase had been in L.A. A post-it note affixed to her dash read: "Better than fishnets. −28." That Chase had signed his note with his uniform number was a testament to his intention. Their arrangement had always been, and always would be, a business transaction. Nothing more.

"Huh," he said, absently, distracted, as if the money to fix her car had been spare change found at the bottom of his washing machine. "Seemed a fair trade for the mashed potatoes."

"Humph." She should fight harder against his help, but she couldn't deny the relief of a real fix. And if he considered it payback for the night with Javier, she supposed it didn't count as him *helping* her, exactly. "Well, thanks."

His free arm slipped around her waist as easily as if they were an old married couple, the type who strolled together in the park and fed pigeons. He felt good—his warmth, his strength. She couldn't get used to that. She wasn't here for long, after all. Leaning on anyone, especially Chase, wasn't allowed. She stepped away.

Just in time, too.

"What in the hell is this?" Tarek called. He rounded the kitchen column, already the loudest at the party, holding the lust jar in his hand. Half a dozen other teammates gathered around.

Chase gestured for her to explain.

"It's like a swear jar. For lusty thoughts."

"Many of those floating around here?"

"Gotta be thirty bucks in there so far," said Nunzio. "Count that shit, man."

Wilcox did the honors.

"Thirty-six lusty thoughts."

Thirty-six? Wait. She may not have an MBA in restaurant management, but she was queen of budgeting and watching every dollar. Thirty-six was a lot more than she had contributed. Willow glanced at Chase, her pulse quickening. She tried to convince herself his lusty thoughts had been about his date. But she wasn't very credible.

"That's a lot of damned lust around here," said Tarek, his suspicious gaze aimed directly at her.

Her turn to squirm. Too bad the gumbo had been stirred to oblivion.

"Well, his underwear ad is on the billboard visible from the terrace. I have a pulse, you know."

Cat-calls. Hoots. Assorted guy-animal noises. Platter of cornbread in hand, she headed out to the dining room to add it to the buffet. She really needed to stop being so honest.

The last of the team left near midnight. After they put away enough food to fuel the next three games and lobbed endless compliments her way about the food in the way only guys can—body noises and groans and enough curses to put Estelle to shame—they had put Willow in a recliner and formed an assembly line to clean up the kitchen. The spectacle was more entertaining than the impromptu sing-along Booth had started when the television accidentally landed on the karaoke channel. She giggled and sank into the supple leather and tried to take a mental snap of the moment. Before long, she would be living hand-to-mouth again because there would always be someone who needed money more.

When clean-up was finished, they had settled in for a competitive session of a pre-market NBA game on the video console. Four brothers hadn't only prepared Willow for live hoops, but she had long ago mastered the art of digital sports games. She proved better at being Tarek than Tarek, himself, to the endless delight of everyone assembled. She, along with Wilcox and Rogers, took the Bill Walton-era Trailblazers to the finals. On repeated protests for a rematch, they trickled home a few at a time until Chase said the last of his good-nights and closed the door.

Willow curled up on the couch and yawned. The day had slipped away, stealthily and seductively comfortable. She reminded herself not to get used to it. Reality had a way of smacking her in the face when she took her eye off the ball. Or in her case, balls, all moving in different directions.

Chase settled beside her. After a day of raucous conversation and loud egos, the silence was welcome and strangely not awkward. Even she didn't have much to say at that moment. His knees were wide, relaxed; his movements were unhurried, comfortable. He picked up a video game controller and fired up a pre-release NBA game.

"One more game before we call it a night? I need to unwind. Let's see what you can do, Trick Shot."

Straight up, she would have staked Estelle's bingo money that he was flirting with her. Her blood heated.

"You're on. You pick first."

"I'll be the Kings." He scrolled through the menu and selected their checkerboard alternate jerseys.

"Feeling nostalgic?"

"A bit."

Something in his voice gave her pause. "So long as it's not regret. Just remember, you miss all the shots you don't take." She scrolled through the menus until she landed on her selection—current Alloy's season line up, special-edition Latino jerseys—before she realized he had been watching her.

"What?" she asked. "I have a thing for rare jerseys."

"No, it's not that. Someone used to tell me that when I started basketball."

"Smart someone."

"Yeah, he was." His tone was sad, reflective.

The starting buzzer sounded.

Willow won the tip-off. She pushed the button on her controller to call a time out.

"Seriously?" Chase said.

She bit her bottom lip. With a few deft menu moves, she traded number 28, Chase Holbrook, for some no-name scrub on the Miami Heat.

"Hey!"

"I just don't think he lives up to the hype," she said. "I don't think he's the stud everyone seems to think he is."

"Allow me to demonstrate," he said with a sly smile. And he pounced.

Her attempt to keep from dissolving into laughter proved futile when Chase grabbed for her controller, trapping her against the arm of the couch. She squirmed and writhed for her freedom, nearly sliding off the worn, leather fabric. He caught her before she reached the floor and scooped her back onto the sofa.

Under him.

Hands braced on either side of her head, knees astride her hips.

Breathing fast and hard.

They froze. She watched his eyes darken with desire as he processed their compromising position. He made no move to release, to back-track, to do anything but study her face as if he was looking for answers, encouragement, disgust, something.

Willow didn't know what to give him; she wasn't sure herself. Her body was as hot as a pot prepped for a crawfish boil, but her mind telegraphed a clear warning: Chase Holbrook, different woman every few days; Chase Holbrook, supposed to be celibate; Chase Holbrook, will hurt you.

"You are the most beautiful woman I've ever seen," he said softly, his eyes finally darting from her face and down her body.

She didn't have time to laugh, because the moment he lowered his lips to hers and claimed them, reason ceased to matter.

9

____

Willow had imagined Chase's kiss before—strong and steady, not given to showy moves or unnecessary risks, his play on the court but better. He would taste exceptional, unattainable, like a forbidden fruit meant only for a select few, and he would show the same commitment to the moment as he did to his game. She had imagined his kiss before, but all those fantasies were pre-season.

Chase's kiss was playoffs-final-minute-before-the-buzzer intense.

She answered him with two years of pent-up longing. Arms looped around his neck, she parted her lips to welcome him inside her mouth. He might have seized the opportunity of her legs between his, her body completely at his mercy. He didn't. The exquisite and thorough exploration of lips remained their only contact, as if he, too, was taking the time to convince himself this was real, this was happening, this could happen.

As much as Willow wanted him to unpin her and make better use of his hands, as much as she wanted him to find other, more desperate areas for him to kiss, as much as she had played this fantasy in her girly moments of self-gratification, Willow wanted to keep her word more. Her spoken word to Tarek and Chase that she would be a steward of her role. Her unspoken word to Dylan that she would ensure Chase Holbrook had the composition of a man, not an ego, and that the bet money would be hers so that it could be Dylan's.

Around his very deft, very sensual tongue, she whispered his name.

When he didn't respond with anything but a more thorough lip-examination using delicious scrapes of his perfect teeth, she added, "There isn't enough space in the lust jar for this."

Humor was her last defense. But with each successive plunge of his tongue, her defenses subsided. Dear God, she was in trouble.

"Forty-four points." Maybe basketball would get through to him.

His kiss subsided like a changing tide, barely perceptible but for the recovery of his breath against hers. He broke contact and searched her eyes. She knew he was in a vulnerable place, wanting to save face.

"The bet." He sounded vague, only half present, as if his own words hadn't quite penetrated. He licked his lips, and his gaze drifted from her eyes to her mouth.

"The bet. A celi-bet, remember?"

"Right." He rubbed his lips together, backed away, and settled against the cushion behind her legs. He lifted her legs and put them across his lap. Like an old married couple.

She straightened her T-shirt where it had ridden up in a glee-run for bra-fastener highway.

"I don't make nearly enough as Bolt to cover the last three minutes."

"Willow..."

She was trying here. But he didn't smile. He had the glazed look of a motorist who had just veered wildly to avoid a collision. So the jokes were misfiring. She took a stab at honesty.

"I'm here for a reason, Chase. I have to respect that and your hospitality. You're you, and I'm me. Your world isn't my world, and in a few games, you'll be the leading offensive scorer in the NBA, and I'll still be the mascot girl who smells like sweaty balls."

This…this hinted at a laugh.

But he looked over at her and sobered. "This isn't over. I get it—you have to see this through. I'm sure you've already decided who you're going to help with that 10K, and I don't want to get in the way of that. But the moment this bet is settled, Willow, I'm coming for you. Count on it."

Henry Lorenz had the worst layup form in the history of the game. When he didn't look like he was fleeing a wildfire, the wrong knee would pop up or his body would topple wildly off-balance. But damned if his shot percentage didn't rival Chase's today. Henry's game was on-point. Or Chase's was off. Way off.

"Alloys gonna cut your ass if you play like this tomorrow," said Henry, winded. He had the lumbering stance of someone who passed most of his days in a fight cage or humping a boxing bag, but he was the one from Sol's brotherhood of three who remained closest to the streets, closest to keeping it real after their mentor had passed away. "Why you so distracted?"

Called out on his sub-par play, Chase fired his jets, passed the ball to himself via a bank off the backboard and attacked a rebound. Drain. End of discussion.

As much as Chase liked the team concept, basketball was never more alive than when he laid it out in a one-on-one matchup with Henry— two opponents, one goal. On the same outside post in which he cut his game teeth. Sol's gym was Chase's ultimate reset button. Most of the day, it had been about the kids—giving back, asking after them the way Sol would have wanted. Now? Forget it. The neighborhood, the team, the city, life simply dropped away. He wanted his game pure, untainted.

"Nothing, man. Let's play."

"Bullshit." Henry hijacked the ball, wasting time on behind-the-back dribbles, probably to catch his breath. Guy was two-hundred percent lean muscle, but his cardio was shit. "It's this bachelor crap. Pretty boy's getting in his own way."

Chase took the dis as an invitation to pretty-boy all over his ass. He stole the ball and dunked it. Henry went on.

"Serious. I can't turn on one news broadcast without seeing your ugly mug. You got half the women in the city with damp panties. Bound to mess with priorities. You've worked too hard to foul out now."

"It's not like that. I went Father Arnaud last week." Their code for no sex. Father Arnaud had been a French import of the Catholic Church in the heart of Pittsburgh when they were teenagers. While Sol had a drawer in his desk known to all the boys as the raincoat drawer, Arnaud tried in vain to convince them that their gifts were best kept behind closed zippers.

When Chase passed Henry the ball, he sat on it. His exhales still emerged in fast vapor clouds. "If Marcus were here, you'd tell him."

"Get off. I wouldn't."

This had always been a sore spot for Henry. Marcus and Chase went pro, had more in common, saw each other more—at least, before Chase moved back to Pittsburgh—and had the funds to travel and live the same lifestyle. Henry had stayed close to Sol and Irma, to the gym that had brought them together, the martyr of the group. No education.

Just his fists and a mild level of success on the fight circuit. Each one had their righteousness about something, but Chase never once considered Henry anything but his equal. Now he had the chance to prove it.

Chase lay on the concrete court, knees up, his hoodie bunched at his neck like a pillow. Typical Pittsburgh sky in winter: muted blue, no clouds, cold as death.

"It's a woman."

"Knew it. Which Hollywood girl this week?"

"None of them. This girl's completely different. She's Irma, man."

"Ain't no one Irma."

"This girl…she's close. She's got nothing. As far as I can tell, she comes from nothing."

"Gotta watch out for those, man. See you and your ninety mil coming a mile away."

"Thing is, she doesn't care. We had an arrangement. Ten grand for a favor. I put the money in an envelope on the table. It's still there next to coupons she clipped out of the paper for diapers to take to the women's shelter. I wrote a note on the envelope last night—why haven't you taken this? This morning, she had written back—favor isn't finished. And she hates when I try to give her anything. Groused at me for helping get her car repaired the other day. Never once has she apologized for who she is. It's fucking intoxicating."

"Just don't let her intoxicate your ass out of the game."

They talked about the next game against Miami, Marcus's shoulder injury, the city putting eminent domain pressure on the very block they occupied. The time was good—he rarely took it with Henry anymore—but Chase's blood had cooled and he needed to head home.

A standing shadow eclipsed the dusky sky.

Henry and Chase glanced back at the same time.

Willow stood in medical scrubs and a sweater, her arms wrapped around her body in the chill. His gaze ascended to her lips. Lips he had claimed. Lips that were like his favorite candy—the kind that would haunt his system all day if he consumed too much.

Chase's heart staggered out of rhythm.

"They told me I would find you out here."

He opened his mouth to respond, but Henry beat him to it. With more energy than Chase had squeezed out of him the whole game, Henry bounded to his feet and scooped Willow up into a full-body hug.

"Hey you. Been too long. Is it free clinic day?"

"Third Thursday of every month."

Had Chase not already been on the ground, his body would have plummeted on mental impact. That she was here—no doubt the reason she gave him her blessing to head to Sol's gym unmonitored— that she was comfortable with Henry in a way Chase had yet to feel her against him, that she continued to surprise him with infinite layers of knowing everyone and being everything to everyone left him without words.

"Wil, I'd like you to meet my good friend, Chase."

Chase felt Willow's smile all the way to his toes. Secret. Conspiratorial. Somehow more than what she had just given freely to Henry. The gesture edged him back from the toxin that had settled in his chest— whatever the fuck it was. Irritation, protectiveness. Jealousy.

Shit.

"We've met, silly," she said to Henry.

Henry's face pinched. "Right. Bolt. Sorry. So how long are you here?"

"Just finished up. Girls aren't here today, so I'm headed home."

The word "home"—*his* home—dropping so effortlessly from her lips, did crazy things to his gut. Jesus, if this encounter was a three-count tap out, he'd already be on two. He had yet to determine exactly when Willow had transitioned in his thoughts from pain-in-the-ass to jump-her-ass, but he guessed it was right about the time she wore a skin-tight shirt with a crawfish on her right breast and wiggled up on his counter to let him inside her menagerie world for the umpteenth time. Father Arnaud was backfiring. And Willow occupied his mind because she occupied his place. Simple as that. If he wasn't careful, Lawd yeah, he'd be the cray one.

Henry tried to bait her with a dinner offer—some place that was, supposedly, her favorite fusion restaurant.

"Thanks, anyway. I have an important commitment." Her gaze trickled to Chase. "Next time."

She hugged Henry, wrapped her sweater tighter around herself and headed back inside the gymnasium. The two childhood friends looked after her until she had disappeared.

Henry chest-passed the ball. Hard. "Now that, my friend, is an Irma."

Willow had to back out of being bet monitor.

She lay on Estelle's ugly couch, dressed as a scrum—messy bun hair, un-showered, caramel popcorn between her molars. Estelle's rabbit-eared television picked up the Alloys-Heat game but the reception looked like it had been flown in on a sea pelican with a transmitter strapped to its back. At times, Tarek looked like a character out of *Monsters, Inc.*—stretched tall, animated eyes. Chase? Still looked perfect. Even through the blips.

Willow *had* to back out of bet monitor.

She smeared Bludgeoned Hearts polish on her toenails—a saucy, deep-red nod to all the single women out there with unattainable Chase Holbrooks in their lives—and ear-tested the excuses she would tell him.

"My life is just too crazy to babysit an athlete."

"It isn't you. It's me."

Ugh. Like she hadn't heard that odious line before.

"Our lifestyles are incompatible. But I know an octogenarian who would get all up in your wealth."

"Why don't you just try the truth?" Estelle stomped into the room and plopped unceremoniously into her rainbow afghan-covered recliner.

"All right." Willow straightened her spine and summoned something that would knock Estelle for a loop so she would stop butting in. "As much as I loved your erection pressed against my thigh and your examination of my tonsils that rivaled my oral surgeon, a man doesn't change. Especially if he's wearing leopard-patterned Magnum boxer briefs."

Estelle barely flinched. This was the woman who had a torrid affair with Liam Neeson's body double. "Better."

But not really the truth. The truth would be "If I hang around you for much longer, your chances of winning the bet are going out the window." But she couldn't tell him how much she wanted him. She couldn't quite believe she did. The ego-fueled playboy and her? They'd never survive as a couple.

She ignored the little voice in the back of her head that chanted *He's not like that. He's not like that.*

Willow sighed. Her life would spin out of control without Estelle's stable, sourpuss presence. The woman had been in her life since forever. She had taught her the beauty of candor and friendship and service to others. Which was why Willow had stopped to visit Estelle's landlord on her way over and paid two months of back rent out of her most recent paycheck. The only thing Willow could afford to eat now was her fingernails, and there was no way she would invade Chase's pantry. Thus, soup at Estelle's for dinner.

"Men are seasons in your life, Willow. Some are summer—hot and sweaty, seemingly endless nights. Some are the excitement and newness of spring or the fleeting, elusive nature of fall. And then there are winters."

"Cold and detached?"

"In Pittsburgh? Unwavering. Lasting."

"Your point?"

"It's okay to enjoy the summer every now and then."

"Like your Irishman?"

Estelle flashed what few teeth she could still claim.

"I want all seasons. I want what Mom and Dad have."

Estelle's stare grew weary, nothing at all to do with the abnormally high turnover rate on the part of the Alloys' offense. "Ah, yes. As rare as your underwear player missing a free-throw."

Willow smiled. Estelle's mind often failed on all but the essentials.

"I'll let you in on a secret. They, too, had their seasons."

The cheese puffs bloated in Willow's stomach. She analyzed this news in her mind. Apart from the rare argument of Dad not entirely standing up to his family regarding Mom's wishes, they were iconic, granite, flirty summer and stable winters and everything in between.

"Estelle...what aren't you telling me?" Cheese powder caked her throat dry, lodging scud around her words.

"Your mother showed up on my doorstep not long after you were born, four boys and a baby in-tow. Said she was done, that they had lost who they had been and couldn't find their way back."

"What happened?"

"Two days later, they found it again. What they have is reality, child. Takes work. If you set expectations too high, reality never stands a chance. Hopefulness is good for a while, but it's a lonely place to live out your life."

Estelle had remained single her entire life. Too brazen for a convent, she had curled up in a fantasy world where Irishman left his wife. He never did.

Willow's cell phone rang. Dylan's photo filled the screen. She hesitated to answer, to leave Estelle adrift on a raft of sad memories, but the older woman had already rowed to shore, hollering at the game.

"Ref needs to get a wife so he'll stop screwing us."

Willow bit back a grin and answered the phone.

"You see that bad call on my boy?" said Dylan.

She hadn't. "I know, right?"

"Make any headway on that game? Mike is stoked. Between you and me, he could really use it right now. Got some bad news yesterday."

Willow didn't know if this was code for Dylan getting his news or if there were truly two young men in this world who had just been unfairly screwed out of long, fulfilling lives.

"That sucks, Dylan." For Mike. For you. She needed something to fill the quiet, vampire-ish void that sucked all the life out of the conversation. "I'm looking at the Knicks game coming up."

"Are you serious?" The news kick-started his voice. "I can't wait to tell Mike."

"Let's keep it on the down-low, 'kay? Just until things are solid."

"I got ya. Hey, I miss you."

"I miss you, too, Squirt. Toe a straight line. Do everything your doctors tell you so we can make this happen, yeah?"

"You got it. Tell your boy Holbrook to penetrate more when his threes are missing. It's like he's window-shopping out there past the arc."

Her boy. She felt her cheeks heating up and was grateful this wasn't a video call. "I'll pass it along."

"Love," said Dylan.

"Love."

Willow hung up and thought about the envelope on Chase's dining room table. It was past time to refocus. Finish the bet. Take the money for Dylan. Guard her heart.

She had plans to make, people to help, restaurants to open. None of that included indulging in a summer man in winter.

Near midnight, Walt called Willow to let her know the floor team had flipped from ice to wood in record time. He would wait near the delivery bays to let her in. She asked about his bingo woman. He informed her she had moved on to another guy. Turns out, even women came in seasons.

Willow herself was most likely autumn: fleeting, drifting, ever-changing.

She packed up two servings of her homemade chicken noodle soup and toasted cheese floats she had made for Estelle, grabbed her athletic bag, and headed to the arena. Her gaze lingered on Chase's note affixed to her dash. She should have trashed it, but she liked the wallop of her stomach when it caught her eye, a little like the g-forces on a rollercoaster.

At the arena, she ate soup with Walt, explained to him about the seasons when placating words failed to help—still unsure if she bought the theory—then changed and got to work. She had been thinking about a new routine for days, one that would keep the audience guessing which Alloys player she imitated. Tarek was easy—his signature move after a particularly sweet goal was legendary. Wilcox was the juke master, nearly giving cameramen looking for close-ups whiplash in the process. Booth had a release that looked more like the pointed hands of a diver intent on sailing off a cliff. But Chase? His angle had stumped her for days. He was nothing if not straightforward, and the thought of slipping Bolt into a pair of Magnums was too on-the-nose. She was pretty sure the brand didn't come in tent size, and she had to admit Chase was so much more than an underwear guy.

Two hours later, she had failed to have an epiphany. She decided a long, cool shower and some sleep would clear her mind. Her best Bolt ideas came in transitional moments when she wasn't really thinking about her routine at all. She had just packed her bag and had her practice ball under one arm when a familiar voice cut the stark, sterile hum of the vacant arena.

"Forty-six."

Chase's voice wrapped around her. Though her body was spent, the rich tenor of his declaration was an energy shot injected straight to her heart.

He stood at a distance, half a court, maybe more.

She knew the point tally, of course. Had watched the game until the final buzzer. Forty-six was the number she had predicted when she slipped from under him the previous night. The team charter would have just landed. He wouldn't have even had time to go home.

He had come straight to her.

She didn't know what to say to him anymore—there was such a chasm between intent and want—so she simply repeated his accomplishment.

"Forty-six."

He dropped his duffle on the Alloy's center logo and half-walked, half-jogged to her. With each step, he moved faster, his eyes layered with greater intent. By the time he was within arm's reach, she knew what would happen.

10

_____

Chase's long fingers threaded through her messy hair. He dipped his head as if a powerful thirst had driven him to a wellspring and he fully intended to drink her in. His lips captured hers, no pretense, no excuse, no hesitation.

The kiss was all-consuming. She fell into his fire, forgetting for a moment that she was supposed to be dousing it.

Until he released her. She blinked in the aftermath of a scorched libido.

"Wow."

He laughed and leaned in for another, quicker kiss. "Forget the scoring record. I just achieved the impossible: I left Willow Bend speechless."

She smacked him playfully. "Hey!"

Chase rubbed his arm where she'd hit him. "Easy there. I just had the best string of games in my career. Thank you. I owe it all to you. You shouldn't turn around and injure me."

It was absurd, really. The notion of him crediting her. For what? For her bet-monitoring aptitude? For the meals she left in his oven to fuel his quest for offensive greatness? It wasn't as if she had banked all those shots.

"You're welcome." Her words hung suspended somewhere between statement and question.

"Let me take you to dinner. Or breakfast."

She dribbled her practice ball a couple times, enjoying making him wait. "That's a weird way to ask a lady out."

"Anyone ever describe you as a lady?"

She barked a laugh. She deserved that, she supposed. No, no one had ever described her as a lady. In point of fact, she did a Vanna White move and gestured down her body, pointing out her sports bra and shorts. "I'm not dressed for anything nicer than dumpster diving. Know a good place that's open at this hour?"

"Anyplace that's open at three a.m. won't care what you're wearing. But you haven't agreed yet."

"I don't want you to buy me dinner, Chase."

"Why not? I've heard people who kiss sometimes do share a meal in a restaurant."

She didn't have a good answer for him. Nothing that wouldn't make her sound kind of pitiful and insecure. *I don't fit in at your kind of restaurant. I don't want to get used to the kind of life I have while I'm with you.*

"We just shouldn't. I'm your bet monitor."

"And thorn in my side," Chase said with a sober nod. He strolled toward one of the baskets. "How about a little wager of our own?

When was the last time you played HORSE? If I win, you come eat with me. If you win, name your reward."

Another kiss. Netflix and chill. No, Willow. Stop it!

"Hospital mashed potatoes?"

"I wouldn't mind, though I was thinking something a little higher quality than that. There has to be something around. I'll eat anything."

"Anything?"

Her first thought was hazelnut chocolate-stuffed crepes served on her bare belly.

"Anything that doesn't lose me a bet, warden."

His smile disarmed her. She should maybe review the finer points of the bet. What exactly counted? How far could they go?

"Fine," she said. "Let's play."

"You haven't declared your stakes yet."

"I'm good with eating. My choice of where."

A half hour later, Chase's stomach was growling, telling him to hurry up and win the damn game already. God knew he'd tried, but they each still only had an H. Willow had missed her shot first, when she'd tried to copy his lazy layup. But her height had been an impediment— and maybe the fact that she'd just spent hours rehearsing. He'd gotten his when she had spun around three times before making her shot, a perfect swish. His had missed by a mile, and he'd learned his lesson. Bolt girl always knew how to make him dizzy.

Now he dribbled slowly, contemplating his next move. Three-pointer? Too easy. Hook shot? No. If he wanted to eat any time soon, he had to lay it all on the line. He didn't even care about winning any more, but he also couldn't throw the game. Willow would never stand for it.

"Maybe we should switch to PIG," he said. "This could go on forever."

"If I beat you, will the Alloys sign me as a player?" Willow strutted across the court, arms swinging, in imitation of every pro basketball player ever.

"Next point wins?"

"Wimping out on me, Holbrook?" She grinned. "But I'm good with that. I burned through supper a long time ago."

He went for a dunk. Slammed it. Turned to gloat with his best grin. She did not disappoint. She stood there with her hands on her hips, an amused scowl on her face.

"Cheat."

"It's a perfectly legal shot." Then he realized his mistake. Willow would know exactly where to find the best food available in the middle of the night. She had to win. "If you make this shot, you win. Fair?"

"Fine." She rolled her eyes, and he passed her the ball.

He had to time this perfectly if he didn't want a bloody nose. He visualized it, decided on his best position, and waited, poised to intercept her.

She dribbled. Started her approach. And he swooped in. Caught her at her hips and lifted. Slam dunk.

He let her down slowly, enjoying the feel of her lithe, strong body against his. His cock twitched as she brushed it, and she sucked in a little breath. He didn't let her go, even after her feet touched the floor, just left his hands resting lightly on her hips. She stayed there a long moment, sighed so quietly he was sure she didn't want him to hear, and then stepped away and faced him.

"You win," he said.

"Doesn't count. You helped."

"All we said was you make the shot, you win."

"I didn't make the shot, though. *We* made the shot."

"You think that if that guy you sent to the shelter that first night gets sober, it doesn't count, because he got help?"

"No, but–"

"Or if Javier has a good day after you visit, it doesn't count, because you cheered him up?"

"*We* cheered him up."

"Still counts, though. You made the shot, Willow. I'm starving. Where are we headed?"

"Head in the Flautas."

Chase read the name on the side of the guacamole-green food truck parked near the all-night bars. Beneath the letters, a baby sporting a sombrero rode a street taco like a go-kart. His stomach growled.

"You said anything," Willow reminded him.

"No, yeah. It's great."

"Best tacos in the universe."

"Quite a claim coming from the head of the Gordon Ramsay fan club."

"You're never going to let me forget that, are you?"

"Never."

She rolled her eyes and bounded over to the order window.

He smiled, delighted by every move she made, her endless energy and enthusiasm. He could not wait until this bet was over. But he wouldn't give in before then. He was on a streak, which meant he could change nothing. And she was the secret ingredient to his success. Her positivity. Her magnetism. There was just something about her to made everything click into place. And he was superstitious enough not to mess with a streak. Everything—absolutely everything—had to remain status quo, no matter how much he was tempted to peel back layers that had nothing to do with her selfless personality and everything to do with her tight, compact, thoroughly animated body.

"Willow!" A middle-aged Hispanic man with a horseshoe moustache set down his pen and ticket book and made his way to the truck's door. He bounded out onto the dark street, smooched Willow on both cheeks, and dropped a line of rapid-fire Spanish that Chase was certain not even Sol's Puerto Rican wife could have deciphered.

"Alejandro, meet Chase."

"Nice to meet you, sir." Chase gripped Alejandro's offered hand.

"The Chase? Aya, big fan. Huge."

"Thank you," said Chase. "Willow is a big fan of your food, I hear."

"Best ambassador in the city, this one." Alejandro squeezed Willow in a bear hug. "What can I get you, mi amor? Are you here for dinner or breakfast?"

"Dinner," she said.

"Breakfast," Chase answered at the same time. "*And* dinner."

Chase loved that she tried to pay. How long had it been since that happened? He pushed her hand aside and gave Alejandro a fifty, dropping the change into the tip jar.

They settled side-by-side on a concrete picnic table nearby, a gateway to a larger city park beyond but close enough to the street to be well-lit. It was below freezing, probably mid-twenties, and he was eating tacos out of a truck in the middle of a cold March night in Pittsburgh. Icicles on his ears were a distinct possibility, but he didn't care. He struggled to remember every having better food or company.

Dinner turned out to be three mini street tacos—one shrimp, one chicken, one brisket. Nothing but the freshest ingredients, stuffed to the brim, messy as shit. One bite and Chase was sold. Breakfast was even better—eggs, chorizo, potatoes, and cheese wrapped in a tortilla.

"How did you find this place?"

She took a healthy bite of the beef taco, which led to an avalanche of sour cream sliding down her chin. He pushed away the urge to lick it off. Instead, he reached for a napkin and swiped it away. She barely missed a beat in the conversation. That they had come to this union— so comfortable, so wholly in sync—was as reassuring as it was baffling.

"Alejandro brought his daughter to the free clinic last year. She was struggling to see the board at school. He thought she just needed glasses, but the volunteer doc that day referred them to a specialist. Turns out Miranda has corneal disease. Without an expensive trans-plant, she'll be blind by adulthood. So Alejandro stays open all night, alternating shifts with his son, to make extra money."

Her story felt like a kick to the nuts. Until Willow, he had become desensitized to his wealth. In the eleven short years it took to journey from destitute to privileged, he had thought nothing of four-figure meals, excursions like helicopter tours and private islands, and pricey sneakers that offered no redeeming features but status. If it hadn't been for Sol and Irma, though, Chase could be any one of Willow's charity cases.

Willow must have noticed a shift in his demeanor. "Hey, you okay?"

"Just sucks, you know? I got a haircut yesterday that probably cost more than this guy makes in one night. I feel guilty."

He couldn't believe he had just laid that out there. Willow's unguarded filter, no doubt, rubbing off on him.

"That's not why I tell you these things, Chase. Don't ever apologize for who you are or what you have. You're generous in other ways."

"Like?"

"Inspiration. How many kids do you think you've inspired to work hard, stay on their school teams, dream big?"

"It's basketball."

"And someday, it will be something else. It's a stepping stone to even greater things. People will listen to what you have to say because you were one of the best players the game has ever seen. So make sure you say important things that change the world."

"You're amazing, you know that?" Again with the fucking no filter. It was like one of the tacos had been stuffed with refried truth serum. Honesty on his tongue tasted new. Good. "You're always putting others first. When is it your turn?"

"You sound like my mother—begging me to finish school, finish anything, really."

"Smart someone." He echoed the sentiment she had expressed about Sol's words in an earlier conversation. He knew she caught the reference when she gave his shoulder a shove. Her touch was an oven that radiated heat all over his body.

"I've just always had an intuition about people. We all want the same things in life—security, freedom, love. Some just have a more difficult time reaching them. If I can help people get to theirs then it's a life well-lived. I can stand on my own two feet. It's not fair for me to take help when other people need it more. Maybe my gift isn't nursing or running a weird restaurant but channeling the right kind of help to the right people at the right time."

"And where does this infectious optimism come from?"

"My parents, my brothers, I suppose. One joined the Peace Corps. One's a Jesuit priest. Not everyone is so fortunate to be born into such a great family."

She had all but gift-wrapped an invitation for him to open up. It was natural, to segue into his family now. Her voice contained the slightest bidding: tell someone, tell me.

"Has Henry told you about Sol?"

"A little, maybe. That you and Marcus and Henry were a few of his success stories."

"He watched me in a pickup game. Sent Marcus and Henry in before the other guys could kick my ass for hustling all their money. Told me later he thought I had the best natural touch he'd ever seen, but I wasn't interested in anything past what the game could get me— money. I was a fucking rail. Sol thought I was doing drugs."

"Were you?"

"No. I learned early on I could get more out of people if I wasn't strung out. Sol made me a deal: come to his gym when I wasn't in school, and he would feed me. Three solid meals a day and everything in between. I didn't care much for boxing, and I was freakishly tall, so I stuck to basketball."

"What about your family?"

"Turns out having a son never took priority over their addictions. When I brought them alcohol or cigarettes, I was their golden boy—

could do no wrong. But it never lasted. They'd get it in their head I'd done something wrong, and I would ceased to exist. When I was ten, they were busted for possession with intent to sell. Child protective services gave me to my grandparents."

"That must have provided some stability."

"In some ways. But they were old and not very well. They loved me but had no means to provide for me. When they died, Sol and his wife took me in. I saw what they did for Marcus—getting him out, getting him to the pros. I thought maybe they could do the same for me. It was never really about the game. Basketball was always a means to an end. Getting out of that cycle of poverty, you know."

"And what about now? What's your end?"

Chase had no answer for her, so he finished his final bite and looked out across the city. Not once had he stopped to think about what came after his record.

"Want to know what I think?" she asked.

"Somehow, I think you'll tell me anyway."

He mentally braced himself. Thought she might tell him that he had never stopped trying to prove himself, to win favor—his parents, his coaches, the fans, the media. Though she'd be right, he didn't want to hear it because head games like that had no end. When was good ever good enough? Championship ring? Household name?

"I think your end is your true beginning." She tipped her head to rest on his shoulder.

His throat tightened. He had never told another soul—not even Marcus or Henry—that basketball wasn't his passion. It felt like a secret dirtier than his drug phase at fifteen or that he purposely chose to sleep with women to whom he had nothing to prove. As with everything else in his life, he had simply leveraged basketball to get what he wanted.

Sitting beside Willow, he realized just how different she was. He wanted to prove everything to her—that he was so much more than a player and his money. He wanted to prove that he was worthy to be sitting beside her in the freezing cold, sharing a meal, confessing truths.

"Ready to head home?"

"No." Her answer streaked by, impulsive, hasty.

He tipped his forehead close to hers, close enough to inhale her scent. He whispered against her soft hair. "What's going on, Willow?"

He meant between them, but she took the safe route.

"I have a family thing in the morning. Brunch at Eros, that breakfast place in the Strip. You're not likely to get up to anything tonight, and if I go back to…my place, I can drive Estelle, who's kind of an adopted aunt."

"She's willing to get into your van?"

"I drive her car. You can come, if you want. It's just something we do once a month to celebrate things going on in each other's lives."

"And where is your place?" He wondered about her pause when she'd used the phrase earlier, as if she didn't quite know what to call the place where she slept when she wasn't at his apartment. He knew she didn't stay in his place when he was on the road, though he'd told her often enough that she was welcome to. He didn't see the point in moving back and forth. But her stubbornness was unconquerable.

"You can just drive me to the arena. My van is still there."

He snorted. "As if I'd let you go home by yourself. That's no way to treat a lady I've just taken out for dinner-breakfast."

"No one's ever called me a lady."

He laughed and started his car. But instead of the arena, he went the opposite direction, toward his own building.

"Chase…"

"It's closer. Tomorrow's a game day. I'll drive you wherever you want to go in the morning. But tonight, you're mine."

They drove mostly in silence. He didn't trust himself not to put it all out there and see if they could run with it together. He wanted her; wanted to be with her in a way that transcended sex. He thought to tell her that he had never met anyone like her, that her gift was inspiring people, just as much as his, because she was inspiring him. He wanted to confess that he was starting to fall for her.

But he had a sneaking suspicion that if he confessed his feelings for her, she would run faster than the lightning that inspired Bolt's name. There would be time to fall later, after the bet was settled, after they were free of its obligations and limitations. For now, he was just happy to have her close.

11

Willow couldn't seem to breathe normally. *You're mine.* Chase's words echoed in her head and sent heat coiling through her limbs all the way to his building. And his arm around her as they passed his doorman and rode up in the elevator didn't help in the slightest.

She had no idea what time it was at this point, but she counted her tiredness as a blessing. She simply didn't have the energy to do what her body wanted her to do: jump this man's bones, explore his body, spend hours tangling limbs and sheets and other things. No, tonight would be just another night in Chase's guest room, like every other night.

She could convince herself of that until she looked into his face and saw the reflection of her own hunger there. Tacos could satisfy a lot of needs, but not this one.

He unlocked his door and pushed inside. He had his duffle in one hand and her hand in his other. He dropped the bag just inside the door and turned on her, using her body to push the door closed.

"Kiss me," Willow heard herself say, without her conscious permission. Not that she would take the words back.

His lips were cool, satiny, and demanding. Enticing. His tongue teased her, coaxing until she opened to him. She fell into the kiss like a cascade—she couldn't tell where she ended and he began. She wrapped her hands behind his neck, and at the touch, he sighed without breaking the kiss. Somehow, he shifted. Before she knew it, his hands were under her ass and he was lifting her.

This was nothing like when he'd lifted her to make that final shot in their truncated HORSE game. It was only a little bit like when he'd lowered her slowly back to the floor. When she'd felt the beginning of his arousal.

Now she felt the full extent of it.

She wrapped her legs around his waist and nestled more firmly against his hardness. Her panties flooded with moisture. With *wanting*.

He hissed and broke the kiss.

"God, Willow. Let me touch you. So sweet."

"The bet—"

"Means that I can't get off. Doesn't say anything about me getting *you* off." He strode toward his bedroom, her still in his arms. "As long as my dick doesn't get anywhere near your pussy, we're still in it to win it."

We. As if they really were in the bet together. Almost as if he knew how important it was to her, what that ten thousand could do for someone who needed it.

He lowered her onto his bed—pure white sheets and a charcoal-gray duvet—and paused with his hands on the waistband of her shorts.

"May I?" he asked. "Fair warning: once these are off, you're at my mercy."

She shuddered. Then nodded jerkily. Meanwhile, she shoved down the little voice at the back of her mind that tried to protest.

He stripped the shorts and her panties off in one move, taking care of her shoes on his way past her feet. Then he pulled away her T-shirt and sports bra. He looked at her, his eyes floating across her naked body.

"Fuck."

"You can't, remember?" She grinned at him.

"Just watch me."

He stretched out next to her on the bed, still fully clothed, and put one huge hand across her left breast, enveloping it. She arched and pressed against him, her eyes closing at the sensations coursing through her body. Then his mouth found her nipple, and she whimpered.

She couldn't even remember the last time anyone had given her this kind of attention. That little voice she'd squashed earlier piped up again. *Because you haven't let them.* She drop-kicked the voice into the next galaxy, daring it to even try to come back from so far.

She kept her eyes closed and just absorbed Chase's touches, hands and mouth and even the roughness of his clothes as he moved over and around her. He traveled down her body, not missing an inch, a centimeter of her. And all the while, he murmured praise and compliments. Finally, his hands cupped her ass again.

"Such a perfect backside," he said. "Part of me is glad you wear that ridiculous costume, so no one else realizes what a fine ass you have." He raised her hips, and his mouth found her pussy. He nuzzled into her, slurped and hummed. He flicked her clit with his tongue.

She nearly flew off the bed. "Chase!"

"Don't bolt," he teased. "I'm not finished yet."

Pleasure coiled inside her, spiraling out from her center, through her belly and beyond, so tight she knew the world would shatter when it all released.

Chase spread her lower lips with one hand, circled her entrance with a finger, then filled her with it. At the same time, he sucked her clit, pressing it hard with his tongue.

Willow exploded with a wail, all her muscles jerking in quick, desperate spasms. Chase cradled her through the orgasm, his warmth and strength exactly what she needed in this moment. When she lay slack and relaxed, he kissed her.

"I'll be right back," he said, getting up and tucking the duvet around her.

She was asleep before he returned.

Eros was not a typical family gathering place. Likenesses of the Greek god peppered the décor, which led to uncomfortable questions from the under-five crowd. Willow's second cousin, a sex therapist, served up a hearty dish of clinical reality by using the term *penis* and comparing Eros's junk to the pigs in a blanket on the buffet, while Estelle used the term *willy*, which led to confusion on the part of Willow's grandfather, William Bend, III, who believed she was talking to him each time the subject matter arose.

Estelle—always considered family—found endless delight in the diversion.

Willow settled beside the old woman. She'd woken that morning wrapped in Chase's arms—his whole body, really, he was so much bigger than her—and his luxuriously cozy duvet. It took far too long to convince herself to crawl out of bed. In the end, it was only a glance at her phone for the time that was able to spur her to move. She'd rushed to her own room to shower and dress, losing more time as she stood under the streaming water and recalled the events of the night—and morning—that had just passed.

She didn't know how she could feel so satisfied and so guilty at the same time. And what would happen next? Nothing. Nothing *could* happen next. Because he was Chase Holbrook, big man about town, and she was Willow Bend, broke nobody. So she'd called a rideshare and slipped out of Chase's penthouse without waking him.

Estelle had eyed her when Willow had arrived to pick her up as if she knew something had changed, but Willow kept mum as she swapped the van key for the key to Estelle's old Buick.

Now, surrounded by family, it was easier not to think about Chase and the pleasure he'd brought her. As long as she didn't look at the walls.

Instead, she watched Estelle construct her waffle sandwich with the precision of a French chef if not the refinement: over-easy egg, slightly broken; Canadian bacon, Swiss cheese, and spinach. Never mind that she could barely wrap her gums around her morning oatmeal. Estelle's taste buds were as ambitious as Willow's mother's attempt to crack open her only daughter's life and scour for short-comings.

"Sweetheart, the enrollment deadline is in two days. Your father and I wouldn't be doing our jobs if we didn't—"

"Push?"

"Encourage. You've wanted to be a nurse since you threw up on the subway in New York. Froot Loops all over that nice woman's camel hair jacket."

"That wasn't my moment, Ma. That was *your* moment once you found out she was Barbra Streisand's biographer."

"If it isn't nursing, it should be something."

"Why? Why does it have to be something? I'm happy with my life, Ma. I do good things."

"I know you do, honey. It's just that your father and I want you to experience greatness."

"Pretty sure she has that covered," piped Estelle. She tossed out the term willy again, just in case Willow missed her meaning.

Grandpa turned. "Wha—?"

Estelle giggled.

Willow wielded her fork in a mock threat.

"Something of great prominence," her mother continued. "Something the magnitude of which transcends everything that came before in your life."

Estelle choked on her waffle sandwich.

Willow's mother gave the old woman a hearty slap between the shoulder blades to help her dislodge the offending mouthful. Her mother could not have known that her newfound appreciation for meditation and spiritual enlightenment had the power to give an eighty-year-old woman a coronary from innuendo.

"Dear, go get Estelle something more to drink."

Nothing at all to do with the choking. This was code for another mimosa, stat. Estelle floated through most of their family functions on happy juice. Alcohol had a way of numbing the woman's sadness at never having a family of her own.

"No need, Willow. I believe there's a tall glass of water coming." Estelle flashed her jack-o-lantern smile and pointed toward the entrance of their restaurant alcove.

Willow turned and saw Chase standing in a collared, white button-down and gray slacks, hands in his pockets. He gave her a slight wave and a roguish smile but was commandeered by a gaggle of aunts who hadn't the slightest idea who he was past the realization he was here to see Willow, who was notorious for never bringing anyone to their monthly gatherings. They ushered him to a choice seat near the head of the table. Introductions flew.

His wide-eyed gaze tracked to her. He was a little like Eros, all whipped-up desire and confidence, until the tempest whirlwinds—the aunts—had him at their mercy.

She wasn't ready for him to be here, to be part of her family, to be part of her heart—which was her family—but he had sacrificed sleep and game-day ritual to come, and he had never looked more hand-some than he did when he shook Willy's hand.

Willow glanced at Estelle.

"Don't even think about it."

Estelle giggled and wrapped her lips around another bite.

Halfway through the family tale about a fishing expedition in which Willow liberated every last walleye from the cooler, Willow's grand-father asked what Chase did for a living. Before he could answer, they took bets around the table: construction foreman (look at those arms!); fireman; Home Shopping Channel pitchman (have you seen that face? I'd buy anything he's selling); city councilman; physical therapist (look at those arms!).

Not one of them knew who he was beyond a guy named Chase who came here to have breakfast with Willow and her family. Or if they knew, they didn't let on. They welcomed him into their conversation, their lives, taking a genuine interest in things about him that had nothing to do with basketball—his hobbies, favorite wines, places he had traveled, the fertile fields of Iowa when he mentioned having attended college there, and his business degree—which most people forgot on the tide of his basketball success. Mostly, they told stories about the practical jokes between Willow and her brothers, and they celebrated milestones—graduations, births, special school honors, even one of Willow's nephews for starting a donation box at his school for homeless animals. They were warm and funny and grounded. He wasn't sure what else he'd expected. An extraordinary woman like Willow could come from nothing less than an extraordinary family.

When the time had stretched long, he excused himself. At a chorus of disheartened awwws, he informed them he had to go to work, which pleased Willow's father whole-heartedly "after the string of jobless losers she has dated of late."

Chase couldn't resist a grin aimed in her direction at that morsel of insight.

He bid them goodbye, taking special care to hug the woman named Estelle who kept winking at him. Certain she knew his identity but had kept it under wraps, he decided she was Willow's inspiration when it came to her unconventional behavior.

Willow escorted him to the restaurant foyer. When they were out of sight of prying eyes, he grabbed her hand and pulled her close. She had traded in her usual gymnastics clothes and Bolt fur for high boots and a slim skirt. Her hair was wavy and twisted in place on the sides with tiny, glittery pins with clear and brown stones, and she wore just enough makeup to allow the real Willow to shine through.

She had never looked more beautiful.

"You didn't have to come," she said, as if an entire hour later, her eyes still might be lying to her.

"Your family is great."

She rolled her eyes. "They're overwhelming, even for me. But I wouldn't trade them."

Against the backdrop of a rainy glaze that had fallen on the city, she radiated an earthy kindness and authenticity and hope.

"Wait for me after the game."

"Chase, there's something I have to tell you."

"After the game, I'm all yours." He meant it. In all ways, he wanted her. His enhanced performance all those times had nothing to do with celibacy and everything to do with siphoning off those who used him. "I have to go. I'm already late for the team meeting. Forty-eight?"

She seemed to be moving in slow motion. Her smile was languid but tender. "Forty-eight."

Nearby, a restaurant hostess lingered, her gaze repeatedly returning to Chase.

Acutely aware of the public nature of their conversation, he pulled Willow into an embrace. A hint of soft vanilla filled his senses. He wanted to plant a scorching kiss on her, a promise of more to come, but she deserved better than to be kicked around in the media as Chase Holbrook's next plaything.

He slipped away, but not before his vision caught the snap of a cell phone flash.

Willow stacked her belongings by Chase's penthouse door. Why had she brought so much crap? Not only had she not waited for him after the game, she was sneaking out like a coward in the night. She had asked Walt to collect the vendor food, as he sometimes did for her, and take it to the precinct around the corner. The graveyard-shift cops always made sure the food got to the shelter when she couldn't make her rounds. She told herself she just didn't have it in her to wait as Chase had asked, that her time as Bolt drained her and Chase would have extra media interviews after he and Tarek pulled within one game of the offensive record. She told herself that every moment she wasn't with him was one moment closer to his goal and Dylan's money because she was losing all ability to remain neutral where he was concerned.

But those were all half-truths.

Willow stacked her belongings to leave because she never finished. Anything.

She was just making the judgment call to leave Quetz as a parting gift when she heard keys jingle on the other side of the lock. Her limbs froze; her heart leapt in her throat. Chase, here, now, meant coughing up answers she was unprepared to give. Unable to meet his eyes when he came through the door, her gaze drifted across the darkened foyer to his polished tile floor. City lights from his open blinds spilled across the polished surface like a thousand gemstones spilled in a moment of carelessness.

Not unlike her heart would be if she didn't get out of here.

Willow Bend, the girl with nothing to her name but empathy, the girl who burned hot on too many dreams but followed through on none of them, the girl who wore a blue muskrat costume because she was afraid to fail as herself, would never, ever fit into Chase Holbrook's highly focused, high-achieving, gemstone-paved world.

Chase searched the shadows, his movements hurried before he, too, stopped. He straightened to his full, glorious height that nearly eclipsed the moon.

"Willow, what are you…?" He glanced around at his feet then added his duffle to her mountain of belongings. "Are you leaving?"

"Yes."

"Why? Why didn't you wait for me?"

"I can't do this anymore, Chase."

"If this is about the stupid bet…"

"It isn't. Not anymore. I need all the seasons, not just summer. If I stay here, you'll be my summer. A white-hot, sweaty, amazing summer but a fleeting season, nevertheless. Just like your game."

"What are you talking about?"

"This isn't real, Chase. You're photo shoots and trips to Fiji and the lead bachelor story on the gossip mags, and I'm the mascot girl who smells like ball sweat and got evicted because I can't focus on any one thing long enough to make a go of it."

He crossed his arms, as defensive a move as any he had ever displayed on the court. "That why you agreed to this? Because you had nowhere else to go?"

"Yes."

"Where do you go when I'm out of town? I know you don't stay here."

"Estelle's. Treasurer and Lead Historian of the Alloys' Senior Hoops Club."

"She did know who I was."

"The woman sleeps in Magnum underwear."

Chase chuckled. The sound, rich and resonant, released some of the stifling tension. He uncrossed his arms and inched closer.

The vacuum his nearness created in her core suppressed her breath.

"None of those things are me, Willow."

Another step closer, like his pursuit across the court at two a.m., but painstaking, deliberate.

"And the women?"

"Never made me feel like this, like a better person just for being around them."

"That's me. Mother Theresa." Cast-off clothes, mismatched socks, self-haircuts in the mirror. She would never measure up to the exotic, jet-setting women with which Chase aligned himself. Any affection would be strictly charity in comparison.

"Mother Theresa wouldn't have me emptying my wallet in the lust jar over there."

"You added the money after your date with Fallon."

"That money wasn't because of Fallon. And I've added much more than you seem to think. Pretty sure I doubled it this morning, thinking about the sounds you made in my bed last night."

"Yeah?" She kept her voice light, coy, innocent so he would have to go there—reassure her that he desired her.

He reached for her hips, his wide hands firm but agile, and guided her into a union that left no space between them. "Yeah."

His erection, veiled behind the thin, flexible fibers of athletic pants, pressed against her abdomen.

She blocked the urge of her answering heat-seeking apex to scale him like a tree until she found full, blissful alignment. Eyes clenched tight, she reminded herself Chase was a season, nothing more. He had always been a summer. He would always be a summer.

It's okay to enjoy the summer every now and then.

"What about the bet?" She needed that money.

"Fuck the bet. I don't care about that anymore. Not the way I care about you."

She sifted that development through her mind. Tarek wins. Goodbye, ten grand. Goodbye, Dylan. She felt sick. Making this about the money was no different a crime than the shallowness of which she'd accused Chase. She was better than that. If she was going to make a choice here, it couldn't be about the money.

"And your record?"

Chase scooped her up—her, emitting a tiny, surprised yelp, and him, barely breaking breath from her added weight. He placed her on the kitchen counter so they were nose to nose. "Since you, I've played my best ball ever."

"And what about after? What's your end here?"

Willow hoped her meaning was clear. She wouldn't be just another knot on his drawstring.

"Since you, I've lived my best life ever. That won't change with a record." That dimple. Gah. He nuzzled her ear, his voice barely rising above a thought. "Let me put you first. For once in your life, let someone put you first."

The prospect roused her. Sometimes, it was exhausting to think about everyone else, to suppress her needs and wants. Sometimes, she just wanted to be selfish.

It's okay to enjoy the summer every now and then.

Her honorable intent collapsed like a cream puff mixed at conflicting temperatures—her resolve frosty, her body sizzling.

"One request," she said, bashfully biting her lip.

"Anything."

12

———

Actually, she had more than one request. Currently, the list was reproducing like it was on a circular loop. She couldn't stop thinking up new ways she wanted the most beautiful man in the world to put her first. But her numero uno request was of paramount importance.

There was no effing way Willow was checking into Holbrook Hotel and Hump Spa smelling like Bolt. Shower first.

At the prospect of exploring each other first in the shower, Chase stripped off his athletic warm-up jacket, an action she had seen him perform a thousand times courtside. Of course, he usually had a number twenty-eight jersey on underneath. Nope, no jersey this time. Just the close-cropped shrubbery of a manscape, sprouted from smooth, contoured granite.

He wagged his brows as if to say your turn.

"No fair. Show me something I don't see on a commercial every night."

Chase stepped out of his shoe.

"Sock too."

He was trying not to laugh. Really. But he reached down to slip off his athletic sock, lost his balance and had to grab the countertop to right himself. At his smile, locked inside an exquisite frame of nakedness, he could have stuck a nearby fork in her. She was cooked.

"Blood no longer in your ears for balance, eh?"

He wagged his brows, again.

So they were going to do this. Strip in his kitchen. Take turns. Go up in flames.

She removed her ponytail holders and shook out her hair—a complete wreck from sixty-plus minutes inside a fifty-pound costume.

He shook his head. More dimples. Shit. Because brain waves ceased in his nearness, she glanced down at her options: her Elephants Can't Jump basketball shirt, red spandex boy shorts. Literally, nothing else. Blue fur was an inferno made no better with underthings. She reached for the hem of her shirt, Holbrook-style, and went for it.

Chase's eyes went all half-court, blind-folded, win-season-tickets shot. She propped one heel on the granite and arched her back. Provocative couldn't hurt.

In fact, it brought out his best play.

He dropped his pants and Magnums, one sporty maneuver so magnificently executed despite his rather sizeable erection, she thought she might reward his flair with a round of applause. All of her late-night cheese ball raids in front of Estelle's TV had not prepared her for Chase's magnum opus that had always stayed just beyond the camera's lens. She supposed it came with the territory, an athlete so comfortable with what God gave him because part of his job description involved stripping down and suiting up. But damn if he wasn't preening—feet wide as if he had just stepped off a pirate ship, hands slung low and indifferent on his notched hips, a mega-watt smile that would have landed him a toothpaste commercial on a planet with no clothes.

What does one say to perfection? "I'm speechless. Can I just pop some popcorn and watch *The Chase Show*? I've been wanting to see it for so long."

"Not a chance."

"So much for putting my wants first."

She answered him with a bold attempt to mimic his grace, but her shorts were practically painted on. All legs and arms and less-than-dignified wiggles. Once, the back of her hand tagged his silky member.

"For the foul of standing too close to someone exiting spandex, a penalty shot."

A chuckle formed deep in his chest cavity and erupted through his slackened lips. His eyes were heat-glazed on her nether parts. He scooped her in his arms and carried her through the light-dappled shadows to his wing of the penthouse. His fingertips splayed at the side of her left nipple, already swelled and taut from the chill in the air. If a moment of incidental contact could send a jolt of sensuous torment straight to her crux, she might spontaneously combust at his focused game plan.

Already, she was damp.

Through his bedroom, where he'd played her so perfectly, so recently, and into his bathroom. He planted her feet on a white rug that felt like a cloud and reached inside a set of glass double-doors to turn on the hot water spigot. A flick to the switches near the towel rack and the enclosure became the most vibrant display of illuminated, flowing water Willow had ever seen.

"I had no idea what this was. I thought it was a steam room or something." The glass mini-room had no visible shower heads. A lowered black panel in the ceiling rained down fifty streams, collectively wide enough for two. A raised, black-tile block provided seating on one side. Opposite, a curving slab of smooth gray marble invited the occupant to lie down at waist-height while five over-body panels, lit blue, sprayed the length of the shower bed. As if all of that weren't magical enough, a hundred or more mini-lights cored out of the surrounding marble gave the impression of a galaxy of stars.

"It's that, too. Some pros spend their money on cars. I figured that I spend enough time in a shower, I wanted the best."

"You could have a party in here." The moment her words left her mouth, she wanted to scour them from her mind. No doubt, other women have enjoyed this space with him. Maybe at the same time.

As if he could sense where her mind strayed, he stroked her chin and lifted her face to his. His fervent gaze sought hers. "I won't lie and say there haven't been others in here with me. But I'm here with you now because there's no place I'd rather be and no one I'd rather share it with than you."

His hand trailed down her arm and tugged at her fingertips. Colored steam churned like neon thunderclouds out of the glass opening, a gateway to the pleasures that lay beyond, a barrier to the outside world they left behind. Here, in this otherworldly space, there were no delineations of status or fame. They entered the main flow of water as Chase and Willow, two unlikely souls who intersected by circumstance, drawn together out of an intangible something that surpassed mutual respect and fondness.

Water flowed cottony soft against her skin—not at all the stinging sensation of every shower she had ever known. Streams cascaded in rivulets to her scalp, flowed past her hard nipples, and joined with the wetness already present between her legs.

As when he was sweat-soaked in the heat of battle on the court, dripping wet was his most disarming look.

Chase lifted her fingertip to a touch-panel and tapped it. A digital readout added flames or subtracted them, based on the location tapped. He was giving her authority over their pleasure. She loaded up the heat and tugged at his neck so their lips merged.

The bond was tenuous, slippery. Forsaking the natural friction of their earlier kiss, they skated their lips against each other. They explored each other's mouths as if they were hidden grottos sheltered from the rain. His erection twitched and bobbed between them, growing ever-harder with each new erotic exploration: earlobe, neck, collarbone. Down, down, down…

He led her to the bench and encouraged her to sit. After adjusting the spray so that she was warm but not engulfed, he spread her legs wide, knelt, and filled the space before her. He reached for a nearby bottle and pumped out a pearly citrus shampoo then set about lathering her hair and rinsing, stopping every so often to pepper her body with kisses. His hands were gentle; his fingers were long and skillful. Needles of mind-numbing desire penetrated her scalp and ran a course straight for her exposed clit. He reached for a rigid bar of man-soap, label still imprinted at its center, and mapped out a musky-coconut trail over every inch of her skin—shoulders, ankles, and everything in between but the trinity of touchpoints where she most ached to feel his touch.

"Please…"

"Yes?"

"Nipples…"

He leveled her with a wickedly hot smile and teased the rigid bar across the peak of her left nipple. Everything low inside lurched toward him as if he had triggered a magnetic field that could only be neutralized by more touch, harder touch, deeper touch. She arched her back and slid lower, knees wider, her right breast angled for equal attention, inviting him on a moan that filled the glass space when the soap was no longer enough.

He nestled the bar so that it was touching her spread pussy, one short, clipped contact of his fingertips that nearly drizzled her to the shower floor. His lips and fingers and teeth zeroed in on her nipples, each taking turns introducing sensations until waves of heightened pleasure turned to gratifying pain then back to an ecstasy greater than she had ever known.

In a liquid world, she longed for something to ground her against the ecstasy. She reached for his dick the same moment his attentions turned toward her deluged folds. He watched as she cupped the weight of his testicles, massaged their pliable girth then wrapped his shaft in her palm and dished back the same tortured bliss she had endured.

His neck relaxed on his wide shoulders. His head tipped toward the waterfall above. In ecstasy, as in the throes of competition, his brow tensed, his mouth slackened in its hunger for oxygen, and he cursed. Under his breath, walking the tightrope of control, half-groan and half-rasp, he reminded her of their game plan.

"This…oh, fuck…was supposed…to be all you."

"Well, all of me wants to see what happens when you let yourself go."

He filled her grip, his excess demanding more ambitious strokes and the help of her other hand to ensure no part of his manhood was left neglected. Alternating between closed-eyed transcendence and razing stares that were a precursor to hard, ravenous kisses, he lost his ability to kneel before her. He sat back. With his elbows, he braced himself against the pristine shower floor. She stalked him, hands propped on either side of his lean body, from his enormous feet to calves and thighs dusted with hair to a rigidly veined and plum-tipped cock that begged for her mouth.

At lick one, it was word one—her name enfolded on his gravelly tongue. From his soft nest of hair at the base, past his banded ridge to his smooth, weeping peak, she forged a circuitous trail with the tip of her tongue until his penis bobbed in anguish for something more.

Again, he spoke her name, barely audible above the rush of the water. The sound was infinitely erogenous, as if he knew she needed that, needed confirmation that she was not just anyone to him, but someone special. She rewarded him by taking him fully into her mouth until his downy head skimmed the back of her throat, again and again.

At this, he collapsed against the drain and prayed to a holy deity for her to stop, to keep going, to stop, to keep going. When she explored his thickness with her best tongue gymnastics, he reached for her shoulders and hauled her against his chest.

"So very Willow," he said around labored pants. "Always giving."

He helped her to her feet and onto the shower bed. His eyes devoured her body as if she were a carnal buffet. He adjusted the water splashing her, neck to feet so it was a mere trickle of burning-hot water running the lines of her body. He captured her feet, at a loss for where to be, what to do and hooked her heels around and over the shower head panel keeping her awash in light and steam.

After a slippery tug toward the end of the table, she was mercilessly, unabashedly exposed. As vulnerable as she had ever been with anyone.

"Chase…"

He slurped his way back up her body, his lips sipping in the pools at her belly and streams below the swell of her breasts. When he reached her neck and face, he pulled back and drank in her expression. But not for long—his gaze wandered again.

"Hmm?" He had become distracted by her body's angles, stroking his large hands down to where they joined her spread thighs, as if he was working out the perfect man-to-woman play in his mind.

"I liked the soap."

He halted his hand's progress, smiled, and reached for the bar, cast forgotten onto the shower floor. His assets hung heavy and low, adding to the visual ass-banquet from behind.

She giggled. Wasn't that a cardinal rule for athletes?

"You, bending for that soap, is just about the sexiest thing I've ever seen. You're as gorgeous from the back as you are from the front." She was sure he didn't need to hear that—he must have heard it every day of his adult life—but she needed to say it.

He positioned himself at the end of the shower bed she occupied, spread eagle, and trailed circles and squiggly lines of musky-coconut scent along her inner thigh. "And you, sweet Willow, are addictive in every possible way. I've forgotten how to be anything but with you, and the thought of being inside you makes me want to scale these fucking walls."

Willow was glad she was lying down because his bold declaration steamrolled her.

The bar of soap meandered a path lower, lower, until her pubic hairs bogged its progress. When she thought Chase might retreat, give the other thigh the same attention, he surprised her by skipping her mound altogether and using the soap's rigid lines to enter her.

Her muscles clenched around the invasion then relaxed around the source of the thrilling sensation coiling, tightening, lifting her ass greedily from the slick, watery surface to chase more. The bar-fuck transitioned to his fingers, first two then more, until the ache of a fat stretch of her channel nearly engulfed her. And when she would have testified that nothing else he might have done could have felt as heavenly, he dipped his head and sucked her folds into his mouth. With a ferocity that washed her away on a sharp, blissful edge, her body racked into wave after wave of delicious torment. Her floodgates opened and her moisture joined the water sluicing over her throbbing folds.

When she opened her eyes and returned to the moment, this place, she flushed at how quickly she had reached orgasm. How woefully inexperienced he must think her. Water splattered her open lips, and she gasped for air, until he was there with a kiss that tasted like musk and coconut and the tinge of a new flavor she knew to be her. She was grateful for the water to hide the silly tear of joy that sprouted in her eyes and charged down her temple.

"Thank you."

He smiled. She was pretty sure he laughed, too. Mostly, he kissed her and inspired thoughts of other, better ways to thank him.

"My turn for a request."

"Anything."

He reached for the shower's main controls and shut off the water. Steam crowded them, the heat cloud wrapping their nakedness until it was nearly unbearable.

Door propped open, he reached for a long, terry-white towel on a nearby warming rack and wrapped it around her. With another, he patted and wrung out her dripping hair, then he slung the towel low around his hips.

"Wait here."

His soft command heated her more than the towel. He returned with a fresh number twenty-eight jersey and an explanation poised on his tongue.

"I've wanted to see you in this—only this—since the night you wore Tarek's number. No one else has ever worn mine."

"Original?"

"Team-issued."

"What if I come all over it?"

He barked out a laugh, his eyes glistening with surprise. "Then we'll wash it in the shower, together."

She dropped the towel and slinked into his uniform. He gathered the armholes front and center and hooked them around her cleavage so that both breasts hung from the openings.

"Now it's fucking perfect."

He grasped her breasts with both hands and squeezed them together, high, extreme, fully erotic. She backed against the bathroom wall and hooked a leg up over his hips. They mimicked the dance of penetration, his length seeking, probing. It would have been so easy for him to drive straight into her.

He didn't.

"Fuck!" His voice was bereft with intense need. "I want to enter you so fucking bad right now, but I know what you must think of me. I need you to trust me. I would never do anything to hurt you."

He had lost her. She wasn't sure what he was talking about until he picked her up, caveman-style, and hauled her into the bedroom, his fingers taking the opportunity to piston inside her along the way. He laid her gently on his bed, opened the bedside table, and pulled out a condom packet.

"I'll get tested tomorrow. Prove to you I'm not the reckless playboy the media would have you think. But for now, it's all about you and you deserve to be protected."

Her throat constricted. This was his end game. And it was sublime.

She took the package from him and dressed him for the occasion then teased him just out of reach—standing over him, straddling; off the bed, booty-shaking. It reminded her of putting on a compression sock in nursing school—so tight, so big. He swiped for her in an attempt to grab nipples or ass or wet hair, anything to distract her from her mission. By the time his impressive shaft stretched the rubber to maximum capacity, they had dissolved into the familiar place of Willow and Chase.

Unabashed fun.

Finally, he caught her wrists and tugged her down, backward, her clit hovering just over his face. When she tried to squirm away, he consumed her once more until their laughter died in the wake of a powerful need to finish what they had begun. She hauled herself down his six-pack, nestled the tip of his cock against her opening, wriggled the full hilt of him inside her, and rode him backward.

The stiff angle of his length necessitated a calculated entry, but the reward of his tip against her hyper-sensitive spot more than made up for the limitations in movement. That, and him lifting the hem of his jersey to drop appreciative comments about her fit ass and the erotic view of her lips swallowing him. He might have climaxed then, so expressive were his outbursts, but he lifted her free of him and reminded her that she was his sole focus. As he had with the water, he was giving her the ultimate decision about her pleasure.

There was only one way to leverage all Chase had to offer.

She tugged him off the bed to standing then scaled the high mattress on her hands and knees, wiggling her ass and backing up in invitation.

He needed no guidance to thrust back inside her slick folds. She accepted every relentless inch he had to offer. As he had always been on the court, his rhythm was swift and determined. Blood engorged the tissues surrounding him. Shuddering vibrations scaled her higher, higher, and begged her to let go. When ecstasy broke, he gave a fevered push to his peak, sank into her until she was convinced he had ruined her for any other, and came, joining her with a husky cry that echoed through the darkened penthouse.

They collapsed to the bed. He stayed inside her and curled her to him while they found their breath. One thought came to her, loose on the tongue because she was still in that place of paradise.

"*The Chase Show* is so much better than I imagined."

He chuckled against her ear, pulled her closer, and kissed her shoulder.

"You haven't seen anything until the sequel in the back of the Bus."

13

Rain that night tapped a barely-there rhythm against the window. The reason sleep eluded him.

At least, that's what Chase told himself.

Willow burrowed deeper under the covers beside him. He took her movement as an opportunity to slide his arm free, pull on some shorts, and try to find sleep at the bottom of a glass of milk.

In the kitchen, where he had stripped himself bare—heart, head, everything—he poured a drink and settled on the counter in darkness to watch flakes in their downward spiral on the terrace.

Their time together had been incredible. She was as generous a lover as she was giving in every aspect of her life. He believed, inside her, existed an entire world that would take him a lifetime to discover. A world of depth and color, shades of struggle and joy and mercy, and all the exhilarating chaos of a life fully lived. And as much as he worried that he might quickly drown in that kind of chaos, he worried about something else even more.

Being attached to any one person, any one thing, had never played out well for him. Time and again, those he allowed a permanent piece of him had made it conditional. His parents loved him if he stole a bottle of J.D. for them from the corner store. His grandparents loved him if he didn't remind them of what a failure their son had turned out to be. Sol loved him if he toed the line, studied hard, kept his nose clean. His Iowa coach loved him for bringing them to the Sweet Sixteen two years straight. Coach Perkins loved him because he filled seats. Fans loved him when he led the team to victory and crucified him when he had an off game. Time and again, love had proved elusive, fleeting, based on what he did, not who he was.

And then, there was Willow.

She existed inside a bubble of unconditional love, the likes of which he had never known. No matter how many times she made mistakes, her family was there to pick her up. At the previous night's game, Chase had spotted her mother and father in the stands. They came right before Bolt's big performance between the third and fourth quarters and left as soon as she was done. It was no wonder they didn't know Chase from the other scabs Willow had dated. Not everyone deserved love and acceptance like that.

Certainly not Chase.

A text tone from Willow's cell on the counter snagged him from his thoughts. He shouldn't look. But the rain tapped and the milk had yet to kick in. He gave into temptation.

Dylan

You get close enough to Chase to get that invite yet? Probably like Lebron. Nearly impossible without a death wish. lol.

Milk curdled in Chase's stomach. That someone would make a joke about dying to get close to him. That Willow had any hand in it.

He hopped off the counter, feeling as if he'd gotten a size fourteen sneaker straight to the nuts. Turned out even Willow wanted something from him. Who was this fucking Dylan? Why had Chase been all up in Willow's crazy fucking world for weeks and he'd heard no mention of the guy?

As if on cue, he heard the shhp-shhp-shhp of her unicorn slippers crossing the penthouse tile toward him. He flipped on a single light over the counter.

"Who's Dylan?"

"What?" That one word from her lips had two distinct layers: sleepy and confused.

He slid the phone across the smooth granite toward her. She pressed the home button and scanned the message.

"Chase…"

"Don't fucking *Chase* me. Tell me he's not a boyfriend. Tell me this whole thing wasn't a plan just so some dude named Dylan could meet me. I can't believe you'd do such a thing."

"He's not a boyfriend. But yeah, I accepted the role as your bet monitor just so Dylan could meet you. He's my nephew, and he's in the hospital in New York, dying of cancer. The Make-A-Wish people were going to get him out here, but he gave his wish away to another kid who, he said, needed it more."

"Why didn't you tell me? I met your whole family yesterday, but you've never even mentioned him." Chase didn't know whether to be more or less angry at this revelation. This Willow was the Willow he knew—she hadn't turned into a stranger. But he was pissed that she hadn't explained.

"It's hard to talk about. I feel so…helpless. Plus, I couldn't be sure his visit would even happen. I needed the money from the bet to cover all the costs. And before I talked to you about it…I needed to know more about you. I needed to know for sure you wouldn't let him down." Willow paced the kitchen and avoided his gaze.

"How much longer would you have needed? If I hadn't found this message, forced the issue, what more would it have taken before you were sure? After all this time, everything we've done together, you still don't know enough about me? You still don't trust me? You truly think I might let down a kid? Fuck, Willow. What do I have to do, give away a kidney?"

"It's not like that," she insisted, sounding shaky and apologetic. "I just…I needed to make sure this was just right for Dylan. I had to look out for him. It's my responsibility."

"But why did that mean you couldn't talk to me about it? It's all right to accept help, Willow."

She just shook her head. "I can't."

"You still don't trust me." The revelation hit like a bolt of lightning, jolting through his heart. "I think it's time for you to go," Chase said. He was done with this. If she didn't trust him, how could he trust her? He'd fallen for Willow because she was so open, because she laid it all—he thought—out there. But he'd been wrong. "Take the money on your way out. For Dylan."

Chase stalked to the terrace and punished his barely-clothed body in the cold rain. He wanted numbness to settle in so he didn't have to feel the pickaxe she had wedged in his chest. The numbness came.

The hurt remained.

Chase knew two minutes into the away game in Dallas he was done. The Mavericks' defense out-hustled him, Tarek out-shot him, the net had plastic wrap over the rim on every goddamned jumper, and the rabid home fans in their quest for a playoff slot wormed into his head and crowded out his focus so he couldn't think.

Coach sent him in for the final stretch. Probably as punishment. This time, Chase was on the receiving end of humiliation. No chance to catch up, but something more powerful would happen tonight. Coach kept Tarek on the court, too. No one wanted to sail into the record books from the bench.

Wilcox passed it to Chase on an inbound. Tarek would have his time. Chase just wanted one. more. shot. He tried to pump-fake but the defensive player read his eyes, was younger, faster. Colin Mackley paralleled his rising action and slammed the ball to the court, dishing out a decisive block. The mics near the rim picked up the denial, like nails driven into a coffin. The mics also picked up the collective Oh-s! from the fans. The ball bounced out of bounds. Whistles blew. Chase's gaze drifted to the key.

Tarek had been wide open.

Back home, Chase drilled the ball into the worn paint, set his feet, and executed a near-perfect three-pointer. Net only, no sound. And no one inside Sol's darkened gym but him to acknowledge it.

At least, he thought.

"Best arc in the NBA."

Willow's voice hit him like the ball hit the floor after his shot—a slow, decisive beat that echoed through the hollow spaces of his chest. He hustled after the ball because he didn't want her to see the guy he was before she walked in. The guy who alternated passing tantrums against the concrete walls and sat on the basketball, forehead gripped in his hands.

"You shouldn't be here."

"Henry called me."

"He had no right." Chase banked another close-range shot.

"I'm sorry about the record."

So very Willow. Blunt to a fault. He didn't dignify the statement with an answer. She wouldn't have liked his response. He dribbled. Hard. Established eye contact with her and released a blind shot.

Swish.

His way of proving she had no part in his game, no power over him, whatsoever.

"I feel responsible."

"Don't flatter yourself. Contrary to what your family would have everyone believe, the world doesn't revolve around Willow."

"What's that supposed to mean?"

He propped the ball against his hip. "They have seats most people would kill for yet they come to the game for three minutes to watch their daughter romp around in a fucking costume then leave. What the hell is that?"

"Those three minutes are gymnastics lessons and failed Olympic tryouts and five seasons of mediocre basketball and everything else I have epically failed at."

"So why bother?"

"Because it's important to me." Her words treaded against tears. "It isn't about performing. It's about them supporting me in what I love. That's family."

"Basketball is my family." He chased down the ball, pinned it to the wall, and grabbed his keys. When he turned, she stood alone on the court, fighting for one final shot.

"Fans pay a fortune to come and see you play night after night and that somehow gives you validation. But what really matters is the reason people come to see you. All these people recognize you, but they don't know you. You put up this mask of playboy and bachelor about town to keep people at a distance. To keep them from knowing the real you. The you I fell in love with."

So very Willow. Blunt to a fault.

"Don't…" His voice cracked on the warning. He cleared his throat. "What about you? Are you just pretending all the time, acting the part of being open and giving? Because that's the you *I* fell in love with. Or is it just me you hide from?"

She swiped at her cheek. In the darkness, she might as well have been brushing aside a wayward hair, but he knew she was crying. He had heard it in the distressed notes of her voice.

"I finally know what I want. That didn't change that night you asked me to leave. It still hasn't changed. I want the kind of love that doesn't end with a season."

Fuck. He didn't navigate tears.

"It wasn't the season ending that broke us, Willow."

"People who give unconditional love, through all the mistakes, are the ones who deserve it back. I made a mistake not telling you about Dylan. I'm sorry. Tarek said you were a stand-up guy, but I had to know for sure. Dylan idolizes you, but his heart—the one that's three sizes larger than mine will ever be—can't take another disappointment. I had to find out if Chase Holbrook was worthy of that kind of unconditional love." She removed a piece of paper from her pocket and laid it on the court. "Trust flows two ways. And I just don't know anymore."

Her footfalls subsided until quiet reigned once again.

He waited until she was gone, long gone, then crossed to her offering and picked it up. It was a newspaper article. An obituary.

Javier Christian Villanueva. Presidential whiz-kid. Wearing number twenty-eight jersey in his last picture.

Chase collapsed to the wood and wept.

Estelle's back porch was an unlikely refuge. The legs of the iron patio chair wobbled. The polar west wind skated along the river and curled through the alcove created between neighboring houses. The night was restless with emergency sirens and somewhere, nearby a stray cat had marked its territory.

Willow had mummified herself in a lumpy down comforter and parked where she could see a sliver of the city. Somehow, pulling the icy air into her lungs was a tangible reminder of life and its fragility. She was here. Javier wasn't. Dylan soon wouldn't be. Why was a girl who had nothing to show for this life still here, when others with immense talent, others who had more to offer, were taken too soon? She thought of Chase's success, his singularity of focus. Since the age of fifteen, he had dedicated himself to one thing and one thing only. Maybe that was the key. Pick one thing, forsake all others.

Or maybe the answer was somewhere between the two extremes.

Around midnight, Estelle hobbled out with a cup of abysmal coffee and a sassy mouth.

"You'll catch your death out here." She zipped her old woman marsh-mallow-puff coat and settled into another iron chair beside her.

"Might be an improvement."

"Bite your tongue, young lady. The good Lord may have deemed me too mouthy to serve him as a sister, but that doesn't mean I can't do his work before he calls me home. Life is good. And no man—not even the Chase Holbrooks of the world—are worth believing any different."

"Not even your Liam?"

"Let me tell you something about Liam. I never knew him—the real him—until the moment I stopped expecting him to be perfect."

"Is that the moment you told him goodbye?"

"No. That's the moment I fell in love."

Willow buried her face with the blanket's edge. Mostly, to catch tears before they fell. Again.

"These things have a way about them," Estelle told her.

"Sounds like something my mother would say. I could use a shot of Estelle right now."

"All right. Quit your damned bellyaching, stop feeling sorry for your-self, and consider that you ran this off into the ditch before it had a chance because your expectations are impossible. He'll never be you —which is a damned good thing. The world can't handle more than one of you. Exhausts me just to be around you. But you—he let you get close. I think that deserves some kind of recognition, don't you?"

Willow gave a weak smile.

"Wake up tomorrow with purpose and don't look back."

At the mention of tomorrow, Willow groaned. The wish foundation had come through where she had failed. Day after tomorrow, Dylan would arrive with a medical entourage, expecting the exclusive Chase Holbrook experience. Thomas had called her to let her know that transport on a specialty plane bound for Pittsburgh opened up and everything had been arranged but the one-on-one with Chase. That, they figured, would best come from someone on the inside. How could she tell Dylan she had irrevocably screwed any chance of fulfilling his most important wish?

"I said awful things."

"Then find a way to unsay them."

"How?"

Estelle grunted to standing and kissed Willow on the top of her head. "In a way only you can, my dear. Don't stay out here too long. I've got more important things to do in the morning than to thaw a frozen body."

She left Willow to her thoughts. Chase's words returned to her.

Basketball is my family.

Estelle's words quickly followed.

Wake up tomorrow with purpose and don't look back.

She grabbed her cell off the table and pulled up Bolt's social media account. Six million followers. An adrenaline pump rocketed through her arteries.

In a way only Willow could, it was a start.

14

____

After morning practice, Alloys players spilled into the locker room. Chase stuffed his duffel to head home. Tarek turned off the wall of televisions, plunging the space into rare silence. Fine by him. Since Tarek had shattered the record, Chase had gone on a strict media diet.

The sixteen grown-assed men staring at him with nothing to say proved more troublesome.

Chase's gut dropped to his sneakers.

Booth spun his padded chair around and Nunzio used his seven-foot-one, two- hundred-and-eighty-pound persuasion to make sure Chase took the offered seat. The rest of the team gathered around.

Tarek dropped a stack of hundreds on the carpet's center Alloy's logo. Imprinted on the paper bank band: $10,000.

"What's this?" asked Chase.

"Tainted money, my friend," said Tarek.

"You won the bet, fair and square."

"Doesn't matter. Can't keep it for all the trouble it's caused."

"What are you talking about?"

Rogers stepped forward and dropped a couple of hundreds on the stack. "My part of the bet pool. Day I came here, Willow found my grandmother a wheelchair. She'd always wanted to see me play. Willow stayed with her all day, made sure food services piled up a special plate for her. That's the day the granny cam tradition started. Every time my grandmother came to a game, Willow adopted her, made sure she felt like royalty. That's solid, man."

Rogers took a step back. Wilcox stepped forward and dropped more cash on the pile.

No. No fucking way he was sitting through this. It was too intervention, too blame-game. He tried to stand. "Guys—"

Two of Nunzio's fingers on his shoulder changed his mind. Chase settled back, arms crossed. He didn't have to listen.

"Those anonymous presents wrapped and waiting for us in our lockers on our birthdays?" said Wilcox. "Willow, man. Never none of that store-bought shit. Always something homemade, just for us. Tarek gets a king cake with a baby shoved inside each year. Rogers got a quilt patched with the jerseys of every team he'd ever played for— and that's a fuckin' lotta teams, man. Dude gets traded more than insults at a NASCAR race."

The room filled with chuckles.

"Me?" said Wilcox. "A framed artist's rendering of each of my tats, man. Different one every year—two so far. Each one of them damned personal."

Nunzio followed suit—money and story.

"Year I came here, Willow put on a bachelor's auction. Raised a hundred grand for the flood victims in my hometown. Makes me choke up every damned time I think about it."

The hitch in Nunzio's normally powerful voice caught Chase's ear, and he began listening. Really listening. Twelve more players stepped forward, each dropping a testimonial about Willow's character along with a wad of cash on the pile until Tarek's money had doubled. More than doubled. When everyone had their say, Tarek settled in a backward chair, eye-to-eye with Chase.

"Willow got caught up in it because she was doing what she does best —making the lives of others around her better. And yeah, the way she lives has some drawbacks. She's so used to taking care of everyone else that she doesn't always open up about herself the way she should. But I've seen the way she looks at you, man. And I've seen the way you look at her. There's something there. Something worth fighting for. And I've never known you to just give up--no matter how hard the fight might be."

And in an irritatingly choreographed group move, they bailed. Every last one of them left him alone, feeling like he had consumed the dirty pile of money instead of merely having it dumped at his feet like some sacrificial plea to a goddess who could do no wrong.

He waited for a few minutes. No one returned. He couldn't leave the money there, so he shoved it into a spare duffel.

In an hour's time, he bypassed his Hummer in the secured lot, a few dozen cabs, and a proposition from two college girls for a ride in favor of a walk. A long, wet, cold-as-shit, soul-reaping walk. He had no aim, no direction. Truth told, he hadn't since Willow left. Correction: since he kicked Willow out.

The wind shifted. Chase looked up from his perpetual stare at the icy pavement to see a green truck with a drunk-looking baby on the side. Head in the Flautas.

Alejandro spotted him.

"Aya, number twenty-eight." He exited his truck and gave Chase a handshake-man hug combo that drove away the chill. "You make our city proud. Anything you want, on the house."

"I'll have Willow's favorite."

It was the first time he had uttered her name in days. Her name on his tongue felt foreign, right, and everything in between.

Alejandro prepared him a steaming plate. Chase ate it at the cement picnic table he had shared with her. Best tacos in town, and he couldn't taste them. By the time he had finished all three, he knew what he had to do.

What Willow would do.

More importantly, he realized, what he would do.

Chase pulled out a fat black marker from his bag he carried for autographs and wrote a message on his empty plate. For Miranda. He waited until Alejandro grew busy with customers then placed the duffel containing the money just inside the food truck's door, plate on top, and walked away.

Or maybe he floated. It was a little out-of-body, finding yourself again after losing the one thing you'd wanted for so long. This time, nothing to do with basketball. Everything to do with his end game.

He slipped his cell phone from his pocket and dialed. After asking Tarek to cover for him at the next day's nine a.m. shoot-around, he hailed a cab back to his SUV. One unifying piece of his puzzle remained.

Willow's last-ditch effort at distracting Dylan from his Chase-goal: food coma.

The arena vendors' food was good for nothing if not the tasty, fatty, globular, brain-suckling carbs that could short-circuit nodes of memory in the brain.

Dylan patted his belly. "No way. I won't eat for a week after that team meal."

Tarek had relayed to Dylan their rookie initiation that involved the food services craft table and a six-course meal an hour before play. The story devolved into an appreciative vomit fest, the most delightful part of which for Dylan was the professional name dropping.

"Demarcus Shane yacked?" Dylan had pumped his knees with glee. "Oh my Gooood. That's great."

What was great was Tarek's thorough—and time-consuming—tour of the Alloy's locker room. And though female sports casters had been known to breach the inner sanctum, apparently mascots were strictly off-limits.

"Guy time," said Tarek. "You understand."

He had ushered Dylan away for a workout with the rookies, some free weights, some non-strenuous hoops—free throws, mostly—a coach presentation of a league-authentic jersey with his last name stitched on the back and a ton of other things that testosterone-driven teenagers and athletes bonded over for the two hours they were sequestered.

By comparison, Willow's tour of the staff-only back areas of the arena —including the multi-million-dollar owner's suite—probably ranked just above Dylan's laborious disembarking of his medical plane: release forms, strict instructions, bags of medications which he was to keep on his person at all times, an extra bag of fluids and his introduction to a grouchy nurse escort who looked slightly younger than Estelle.

With two hours to go until tip-off, the kid looked cashed out.

And Willow was out of distractions. Not once had he mentioned his idol. She knew Dylan well enough to know he was being polite. Everyone had already done so much. He didn't want to seem ungrateful.

Dylan lowered himself into a courtside chair. Thomas hovered, as he often did.

"You okay, pal?"

"Sure, Dad. Fine."

Dylan didn't look fine. He looked pale. Gray.

Thomas glanced at Willow. Prominent lines had sprouted in parentheses around his mouth and at the corners of his eyes. Her brother had aged so much since his son's diagnosis. She supposed if Thomas had stayed close to family, his burden wouldn't have been as great. But in New York, he was an island.

Willow embraced him. He squeezed back, lowered his mouth close to her ear, and choked out, barely above a whisper, "Thank you for this."

Waterworks sprouted in her eyes, but she couldn't let Dylan see. Dylan's grouchy nurse saved the day with an emergency tissue tucked in her sleeve. Willow supposed the woman was used to tears on assignments like this. Willow glanced around at her family—all of them, twenty-two in number, including Estelle, gathered for the first time since Christmas, laughing, hugging, enjoying each other in a way they never would again. A gravity of love.

Without a chance at the playoffs, tonight was the final Alloys home game of the season. And Willow's final game as Bolt. If she was working toward a focus, toward her dreams, it couldn't be as a smelly blue muskrat. No one grows up wanting to be a mascot. And it was past time for her to grow up.

Starting now.

She sat beside Dylan and held his hand. "'Sup?"

He flashed a weak smile.

"There's a bed in the training room where Steve Nash napped when Golden State came to play. I can hook you up."

"I'm good."

"Dyl, listen…I know this day isn't everything you wanted…"

"Are you kidding me? It's more than I dreamed."

"But meeting Chase—"

A familiar voice broke into the conversation.

"Didn't quite rank up there with meeting all the Alloys dancers at the same time…"

Her family gathering parted like Moses and the Red Sea. Chase entered the fold in a flurry of handshakes, back pats, and one cheek-kiss for a very flushed Estelle. Willow's chin spilled to her lap like stale popcorn on a buzzer-beater.

Dylan grinned. "Yeah. That was epic. Wait until Mike sees that photo."

Chase and Dylan exchanged a handshake so complex, it could only have been germinated and perfected at another time, in another place.

Her nephew hadn't asked about Chase because they had already met.

Chase's gaze collided with Willow's open-mouthed stare. His lips stretched taut on a quick grin before he refocused on Dylan. That dimple. Gah. Had she blinked, she would have missed it.

"Where is Mike?" Willow asked. "I thought he was coming."

"Chase hooked him up with the Knicks. He's there right now." Dylan held out a photo on his cell phone of Mike with the star forward for the Knicks.

The part of Willow's brain that generated speech failed. Turns out, Chase Holbrook was worthy. The stuff of heroes.

"See you after the game, man? You can be front and center in the media room with me."

Dylan's eyes lit up. "Definitely."

Chase said his goodbyes, reserving one final, indecipherable glance for Willow, then turned and jogged across the court and into the tunnel.

This prompted Estelle to declare, "That man is hotter than the Devil's backside after eating jalapenos."

At which twenty-two relations to the Bend family name laughed until they sprouted more tears, this time of joy.

Chase had been dreading the post-game theatrics. But in the forty-eight hours since Tarek had shattered the offensive ceiling, Chase had come around. Did he wish he was standing in front of the NBA commissioner, on a red carpet rolled out at center court, getting an award? Sure. But if he had to get out-hustled, Chase wouldn't have wanted the honor to go to anyone else. He felt like a proud brother. In many ways, he was.

His gaze drifted courtside. Willow's family packed the first two rows opposite the Alloy's bench. Dylan had the biggest smile of all of them. Chase hadn't been able to give Javier the mega-fan experience, but he hoped, in some small way, making sure Dylan and Mike had their wishes made up for it. Chase swore Dylan to secrecy when, together, they met with a Wish Foundation representative and gave away Dylan's wish a second time.

An arena full of near-deafening cheers went up at the announcement of Tarek's name. Bolt jumped up and down like a blue muskrat with feet springs. Chase clapped and laughed. He didn't know where he stood with Willow, but it felt a little like beginning again, minus the part where he doubled down on the kids and mentally challenged comment.

Tarek went down the line of teammates, shaking hands, embracing. The audience roar subsided. The commissioner spoke again.

"We have one other item of business to take care of tonight. I'd like to ask Chase Holbrook to come to center court."

A stab of uncertainty—something close to panic—seized Chase's lungs. This wasn't part of the team briefing thirty minutes ago. He glanced at the cluster of teammates, those within reach smacking his shoulders, the rest smiling his direction. His legs didn't process what was happening until Tarek joined him.

"Don't keep the Commissioner waiting."

"Is this a prank, dude?"

"No, man. Not this time."

Chase walked from the far end of the team line toward center court. When it took too long, he jogged a bit. The awkward dwindle of audience noise picked up with his increased hustle. He gave a casual wave to the fans. He thought maybe crawling under the red carpet was a good option.

The Commissioner shook his hand. Chase took the space beside him.

"Each year," began the Commissioner, "fans get an opportunity to become involved in the celebration of this great sport by getting one collective vote on the panel of sportswriters and broadcasters representing the United States and Canada. This honor, proudly sponsored by a car company with strong roots right here, in this fine city…

The media screens flashed with reels of sports cars speeding down the highway and a splashy logo. Audience cheers swelled.

Oh, God. Chase glanced at Tarek. His buddy smiled and nodded his head.

"…opens up to voting on the first day of the season and continues right up until the panel convenes. Two days ago, Chase Holbrook was in the running with ten other players around the league for the most number of fan-favorite votes. Then, this happened…"

Lights in the arena went on a slow-dim. The media screens lit with Chase's usual player introduction then segued into a video package he had never seen before. Sound blasted across the arena—a mixture of a slow piano tune and voice-overs.

A wobbly cell phone video played. Javier's face filled the jumbotron. Chase didn't even remember Willow filming.

Instantly, his nose began to sting. *Oh, God, I'm going to lose it right here on national television.*

The home movie transitioned into an interview clip of a woman. The caption read Maria Villanueva, Javier's mother. She talked about her son's final days, how he told everyone who would listen about how Chase Holbrook surprised him in his hospital room and hung out with him all night. Her voice continued to narrate over video of Chase dancing in Bolt's costume, quiet moments of her son and Chase reclined together, watching the Alloys game, and squeezing mashed potatoes through their teeth in tandem.

Laughter rose from the darkened audience. He scanned the stands for Bolt, but the lights were too dim.

Next up, a few of his teammates, ribbing him, giving away his secrets, like drive-thru burger runs in the middle of the night where Chase pays for the next twenty cars and never being able to pass a kids' lemonade stand without stopping and drinking their entire inventory—which someone had caught on camera. They talked about his USO tour the previous year to Afghanistan, along with Marcus and other professional athletes, and flashed photos of him with men and women in uniform.

Then came the interviews.

Grady…

Loretta, the pediatric night nurse…

Sam in a dress…

The Nutty Norwegian, who called him stud and roused a cacophony of whistles and cheers from the female fans.

Clarence "Crazy Jack" Dawson with his shoe story—thankfully, leaving out the part of the discussion about Willow.

Millicent, with her fancy scarf…

A handful of kids from Sol's gym—now Henry's—that Chase mentored…

A woman from the local women's shelter, with an old mayonnaise jar and a story about how she found it in their night drop, filled with money and Chase's collectable player's card.

Dylan and Mike…

Alejandro and his beautiful daughter, who blew a kiss to the camera for Chase…

The video was supreme. Masterfully edited, fancy graphics, spliced with endless photos fans had sent in, perfectly orchestrated with music, worthy of a special feature on ESPN, all working toward an emotional climax.

The music quieted. Javier returned. He talked about his hope that there was basketball in heaven. Maria read a thank you letter Javier wrote to Chase but never got the opportunity to send.

"In heaven, I know you will be part of my love gravity. We can shoot some hoops sometime. I might even beat you. It is heaven, after all. But please no dancing. Never dancing."

The video cut to Chase's best moves in a blue muskrat costume. Again, laughter swelled from the fans. The final clip went out on a black screen, Javier's picture in a number twenty-eight jersey and the opening and closing dates of his life.

When the arena lights went up, Chase was absolutely certain about three things. First, that he had become so swept up in the stories, he had forgotten to keep a check on his emotions and had to swipe at tears lingering on his cheeks. Second, that he didn't need the NBA Commissioner to lean close to his ear and tell him, "They love you, son," because Chase could feel the standing ovation thundering through his entire body—not because he outscored, not because he brought victory, but because of him, Chase, the man he was off the court. And third, that this honor had Willow written all over it.

A spotlight found him. The Commissioner raised his mic and continued when the fan noise died down.

"Two days ago, Chase Holbrook was in the running with ten other players around the league for the most number of fan-favorite votes. Then, this video happened. And it went viral. And now it is my extreme honor to present to you this season's fan-vote for Most Valuable Player."

Cheers exploded.

He handed Chase a plaque, shook his hand. Camera bulbs flashed in his field of vision. Passing out was a distinct possibility. The Commissioner handed Chase his microphone.

"Say a few words, son."

Chase glanced out at twenty-thousand people assembled, at network cameras, at his coach and teammates whistling and cat-calling, Tarek more animated than all the rest. Chase raised the mic to his mouth but couldn't speak. The hesitation whipped the audience into a greater frenzy. He laughed and rested the mic against his jersey. His face grew hot from the lights, from the flush of trying not to lose it on national television. He had zero confidence his voice would be there when he most needed it.

He swallowed the thickness clogging his throat. His brain managed to pump out his thanks to the Commissioner and the league, his fans, the special people in the video and the friends he had made along the way, his coaches and teammates, his fans—again—which incited another rush of cheers. But who he most thought about during his acceptance was the one person without whom none of this was possible.

"I was actually expecting to get up here and make a speech, but this wasn't it. So, I'm just going to keep going a little while, if yinz don't mind." The arena reverberated at his use of the Pittsburgh version of *y'all*. "This is the inaugural year for a new award from the Alloys organization. The Unsung Hero award, voted on by the team, team staff, and arena staff. We had about fifty nominations come in over the last two days, and they were all for the same person, so we didn't bother to hold a vote."

He raised his hand to block the spotlight and searched courtside in vain until one geriatric voice rose above the crowd. "Over here, Magnum!"

Estelle.

Chase laughed and tracked the direction of Estelle's outburst. Twenty rows up, Bolt stood frozen on the aisle steps.

"Bolt, I've never wanted to share the spotlight with your center court antics before, but as you've taught me over the course of the season, there's a first time for everything. Get your furry little self down here."

Music kicked in. The crowd went nuts—standing, craning necks, snapping photos, cheering and talking. At least, that's what it seemed. Chase only had eyes for a furry blue muskrat. When she didn't come down the steps fast enough, he passed the microphone to the commissioner and jogged toward her, meeting her at courtside.

He pulled her onto the court and into the spotlight. Chase knew Willow would adhere to her strict mascot rules. But *he* didn't have to.

He lifted off Bolt's head, revealing a wide-eyed, sweaty Willow. "Chase…"

"Hush." He took the mic back from the commissioner. "You know her as Bolt, but the city knows her as Willow Bend, the person who's always there when anyone need help." He ran through the highlights of their time together. Passing out food. Visiting the hospital. Just talking to the invisible people on the streets. "The award is two-fold— a donation by the Alloys organization, players, and staff to a cause close to the honoree's heart. The Pittsburgh Children's Hospital cancer ward will receive one million dollars in honor of Javier Christian Villanueva, the boy highlighted in that video you just watched. The second part is an award to the honoree herself, in the form of something to make her own dreams come true, for once. The Pittsburgh School of Culinary Arts has awarded Willow Bend, our very own Bolt, a full scholarship to their restaurant management certification course. Keep your eyes open for her Cordial Café to open soon."

Willow's mouth gaped. He put a finger under her chin and pressed up gently, closing it. Then he planted a kiss on her lips. She melted into him—well, as much as she could with a wire cage and a fifty pounds of fake blue hair between them.

The crowd went wild.

The team stormed the court, surrounding them, but Chase and Willow were in a bubble of their own world.

"I love you, Bolt girl."

"I love you too, Magnum."

"How did you pull that off? All that video, finding Clarence…?" he asked.

"My request for stories and video about you from Bolt's social media went viral. Someone at a shelter in L.A. remembered a guy talking about your shoes. And I know a few people who helped me edit it together."

"You know more than a few people."

"True. But there's only one person I want to know right now…"

He smothered her last words on another kiss.

EPILOGUE

Willow snuggled onto Chase's lap wearing his two favorite things.

Her wedding ring, which turned out to be the simple gold band her father had given her mother in their early days before he could afford a diamond. For luck, she had said.

And his jersey. Only his jersey.

She scrolled through the latest NBA game menu, controller in hand. She had a few hours before she had to meet her investors at the Cordial Café, and the last thing on Chase's mind as he swelled beneath her was playing a video game. Still, she insisted as she ground out a torturous wiggle of her bare ass over his fly.

He selected the Sacramento Kings. She selected the Pittsburgh Alloys then promptly traded away number twenty-eight for a rookie from the Lakers.

Chase reached for her sides and tickled her until the controller slipped from her hand—it didn't take long. This time, when she squirmed and writhed for her freedom, nearly sliding off the worn leather fabric, he caught her lips and didn't let her go until they had settled the match-up under the most pleasurable of conditions.

END OF TOP-SCORING PLAYER
SOLOMON PRO ATHLETES BOOK TWO

No More Sidelines, December 22, 2022

Top-Scoring Player, December 29, 2022

Tap Out, January 5, 2023

P.S. Can't get enough football romance? Turn the page for an exclusive free book offer and exclusive extracts from **Tap Out, The SEAL's Pregnant Roommate** and **The Fighter's Fierce Temptation**.

FREE BOOK OFFER

Read FIVE full-length romances by USA Today best-selling author Leslie North for FREE! Over 600+ pages of best-selling romance with hundreds of FIVE STAR REVIEWS!

Sign-up to her mailing list and get your FREE books: www. leslienorthbooks.com/sign-up-for-free-books

THANK YOU!

Thank you so much for purchasing my book. It's hard for me to put into words how much I appreciate my readers. If you enjoyed this book, please remember to leave a review. Reviews are crucial for an author's success and I would greatly appreciate it if you took the time to review the book. I love hearing from you!

You can connect with me on:

goodreads.com/leslienorth

bookbub.com/authors/leslie-north

facebook.com/leslienorthbooks

twitter.com/leslienorthbook

instagram.com/leslienorth_books

ABOUT LESLIE NORTH

Leslie North is the USA Today Bestselling pen name for a critically-acclaimed author of women's contemporary romance and fiction. The anonymity gives her the perfect opportunity to paint with her full artistic palette, especially in the romance and erotic fantasy genres.

Find your next Leslie North book visit LeslieNorthBooks.com or choose:

BY TROPE

BY HERO

PS: Want sneak peeks, giveaways, ARC offers, fun extras and plenty of pictures of bad boys? Join my Facebook group, Leslie's Lovelies!

BLURB

Love scores a knockout blow…

MMA fighter Henry Lorenz relies on discipline and strength to get through life. After inheriting his former mentor's boxing gym, Henry has his hands full running a business and training a troubled teen who reminds him of himself at that age. Then a stubborn and distractingly beautiful social worker walks through the gym doors, turning Henry's life upside down. Now, he's determined to prove to her that there's more to fighting than knowing how to throw a punch.

Maggie Kavanaugh is devoted to protecting kids from the violence of the streets. She wants them to use their brains, not their fists, to get ahead in life. When one of her most talented teens begins training at Henry's gym, Maggie is worried. She'll let the training continue, but she's going to be watching every step of the way. And that means watching the gruff but smoking hot Henry as well…

When a dark moment from Henry's past threatens to come between them, he's torn. Should he keep his secret bottled up inside? Or can he give love a fighting chance?

Grab your copy of *Tap Out*
www.LeslieNorthBooks.com

❧

EXCERPT

Chapter One

Margaret Kavanaugh deliberately parked her rust-speckled sedan beneath the billboard in protest. Crowded with representations of every ethnicity found in the greater Pittsburgh metropolitan area, kids of varying ages all stood behind a smug likeness of the interim mayor —interim because the elected mayor had taken bribes, mayor because politics was the haven of home-grown wolves leading sheep. The peeling billboard lauded the success of the All Children Learn initiative.

Maggie sniffed at the irony. The ever-present decay of what was once a thriving warehouse district did little to dissuade her. She lived it. Every day, by choice, she lived it. For the first September since securing her teaching certificate five years ago, she wasn't inside a classroom. The school climate had been insular and structured, with an in-the-trenches comradery she missed at times. But she had gotten out before the system could choke out the last gasp of optimism inside her. She forged her own path toward making a difference—one that didn't force her to forfeit the talented few for the masses.

She slid her cross-body bag over her head, shot the mayor pro tem rigid double birds and hustled across the street to the non-descript gym housed over a long-abandoned Asian market.

By the time she had skirted the old brick building twice, searching for entry, her arteries were a toxic cocktail of caffeine, frustration, and full-dump adrenaline. Leave it to a fraternal playhouse with a back-alley basketball court to have a secret entry. No wonder the gym had to prey upon the community's vulnerable youth to stay viable. Sol's Gym could use a suppository of business savvy. She intended to tell the owner that. Just as soon as she figured out which steroid-driven Neanderthal was Sol.

Maggie expected a sensory assault—loud, curse-driven beats, a prevailing stench of sweat, the general taste of desperation. What she found was quiet, low-key, antiseptic. Punching bags hung still. Florescent bulbs running the gym's length were dark. A few jet-engine-sized fans circulated the vaguely bleach-scented air.

Of course, it was Monday morning, eight a.m. The kids Sol led astray were—she hoped—in school.

"Can I help you?"

Maggie startled and turned toward the deep voice. Attached to the voice was a man in a full-on business suit. Navy to be exact, set against a crisp, white button-down shirt. His shoulders and chest filled the shirt just to the point of straining the seams. She blinked, momentarily off-balance from the incongruity of the suit. Yeah, it was the suit, not the man inside it that flummoxed her. A tattoo—she couldn't quite tell what it was—covered one side of his neck. His hair was dark, cropped close. Something about the way he stood—relaxed yet wary—suggested he was ready for anything.

"I need to speak to Sol."

Anything except that, apparently. He stiffened and walked away. "He ain't here."

He shed his jacket, revealing more of the neck tattoo. Was that a sun? She tailed him into a back office that looked ransacked, or maybe struck by a tornado. He hung his jacket over the open door to a trophy cabinet filled with tiny brass figurines with their fists raised.

Maggie picked her way past a box filled with blue flyers touting an exhibition fight. "He's interfering with one of my students."

The man continued to strip—his white shirt unbuttoned down to a chest-hugging tank top, shoes kicked into a corner, navy dress socks balled and tossed onto a wooden desk. His muscles bunched and stretched with his movements, every inch of arms sleeved in colorful ink like a Banksy on a sculpted canvas. She'd never liked tattoos, though it seemed everyone was getting them these days. Maybe it was that she couldn't imagine permanently scribing any one philosophy on her skin—she was always seeking growth and change—and anything so permanent couldn't be frivolous. She shook her head, annoyed that she was gawking at the play of this man's tattoos against the rather sinuous muscles beneath instead of focusing on why she came.

"I must insist this Sol fellow stop misleading the boys I'm trying to guide to a better life with visions of a glorious career that's nothing but harmful—possibly deadly—and distracting them from their academic obligations."

"And what boys might those be?"

"For starters, Roosevelt Ware."

"Roosevelt?" The man stopped the unbuttoning of his cuffs and leveled her with a direct, contorted stare as if the word had confused him.

"As in the thirty-second president?" she added.

"You mean the one who called pacifists 'sissies'?"

Inwardly, she cringed. "History buff and Neanderthal. This day is a study in contradictions, isn't it?"

He reached for the button at his waist.

"Ho," she turned away. "Do you always greet patrons with a strip show?"

"Only the obnoxious ones. And you're not a patron. Get out."

She sucked oxygen in through her rigid nostrils. The fan at the corner of his office assaulted her with stale air and fed her pieces of her own hair. With an angry flick, she scooped the offending locks out of her mouth. "Just tell me where I can find Sol."

"'Bout five miles down the road. Six feet under. Headstone with the sculpted boxing gloves. Can't miss it."

Maggie felt a twinge in her abdomen, not as much as it should have been because he was so cavalier about death. Her mom and dad would want her to be the kind of person to say something courteous. She chanced a peek behind her. The man was changing his pants.

"I'm sorry for your loss."

"I'm sorry I'm not him right now. At least he's getting some goddamned peace."

Maggie spun. She didn't care that she caught sight of his bulging and rather substantial altogether covered in a thin layer of cotton before the waistband of his warm-up pants settled at his hips. "I don't pretend to know how much of your brain is left since you started out in this…this crass waste of time you call a sport, but Roosevelt is intelligent, gifted in spatial awareness and physics and the intricacies of calculus, brilliant even, as close to a genius as I have ever known. He has the capacity to be something in this life, something important, and I don't intend to allow his talents to slip through society's fingers because some testosteroned oaf sold him a bag of goods about the glorious life of a prize fighter, which will only leave him permanently incapacitated."

He slung his hands low on his hips, staring at her, open-mouthed, mute. She wondered if he had as much going on between his ears at that moment as he did from the neck down. The guy was as brick-solid as the turn-of-the-century structure surrounding them.

She rushed on. "Roosevelt has the opportunity to build a scale model of one of the most important bridges ever conceptualized—longer than Pontchartrain, more creative than the Malaysian sky bridge, more iconic than the Golden Gate. He has the opportunity to get a full-ride scholarship to one of the premier architectural engineering programs in the world—but he can't do that if his hands are stuffed into padded gloves, punching the snot out of a stuffed bag every day after school or getting his own stuffing punched out."

Her lungs were spent, discharged. She gulped greedily for air, her chest rising and falling while she ticked away seconds, waiting for him to say something—anything.

He adjusted himself.

She couldn't tell if it was a gather-the-boys-in-the-neighborhood-after-dressing kind of adjustment or a suck-this kind of adjustment. The fact that she was mentally debating something so vulgar under-scored her point precisely. This environment was offensive. Period.

"Aren't you going to say anything?"

Zero ticks of his facial muscles. Zero expression. "Nope."

The fire burn inside her fizzled to a thin stream of smoke.

"Great. That's just fantastic. You have the future here, in your hands like malleable clay and 'nope' is all you've got." She turned to go, but not before she added one thought. "If Roosevelt shows up here again, tell him to go home and crack a book instead of someone's face."

"Roosevelt shows up here again, same as any other kid, I ain't turning him away."

His ain't wriggled beneath her skin and held her rebuttal hostage. There was no reasoning with ain't. She stormed past a very tall man on the way out—athletic but not at all the physique of a fighter.

"Do yourself a favor and leave before you become a ball-scratching heathen with half a brain cell left to your name."

Only trouble? She couldn't find the door. Again. She didn't know the secret exit of the fraternal order of barbarians, so she spent two full minutes feeling like an exhibition before she charged back into sunlight under the laughing smile of the mayor.

Grab your copy of *Tap Out*
www.LeslieNorthBooks.com

The SEAL's Pregnant Roommate

BLURB

Can these two lonely souls catch a lucky break in love?

Harley Von's never been lucky in life, let alone in love. And her streak of ill fortune continues when her long-lost brother passes away just as they were on the verge of reconnecting. On the run from a bad relationship, she's less than delighted to find herself sharing Sebastian's fixer-upper with his gruff but gorgeous friend, Garrett. With her ex breathing down her neck and a baby on the way, Harley's got plenty to deal with. Falling for a sexy SEAL isn't part of her plan.

Navy SEAL Garrett Moore isn't looking for romance. His life is the SEALs, end of discussion. Still, grieving and guilt-ridden over his teammate's death, he's determined to do what he can to help Sebastian's sister. And Harley's combination of vulnerability and determination is captivating. She's like a skittish fawn refusing to back down from a mountain lion.

He can't help feeling protective of her, especially when the ex shows up and gets physical. But Garrett's only in town for as long as it takes to repair the old house.

Love has a funny way of changing things, though.

**Grab your copy of *The SEAL's Pregnant Roommate*
www.LeslieNorthBooks.com**

BLURB

Alice hates fighters.

They're arrogant, broody, and have an ego to match their hulking muscles. Not to mention her scumbag ex was one of them..

But when her dad, a legendary MMA trainer, suffers a stroke and the medical bills start piling up, she's forced to start training one of the infamous Burton Brothers. All she needs to do is pretend to be her dad for a few days. But from the moment Bryant Burton shows up at the gym, all bets are off. With his taut muscles, steely gray eyes, and simmering strength, fighting his pull is going to be the biggest challenge of all.

Bryant can't understand his cravings. If the desire he's feeling for "Coach Anders" wasn't disturbing enough, the man's daughter is starting to make him forget why he came. Her creamy skin, petite body, and full lips are driving him insane with need. And the fact she keeps disappearing doesn't help either. If he's going to be ready for his championship fight, he'll have to do something to satisfy his urges and get his head back in the ring.

One kiss is all it takes to ignite their chemistry, but with Alice's deception and Bryant's short fuse, things are bound to go up in flames...

The BADDEST boys on the planet have finally met their match...

Grab your copy of *The Fighter's Fierce Temptation* (The Burton Brothers Series Book One) from www.LeslieNorthBooks.com

EXCERPT

Chapter One

Time. Therapy. Healing.

Those words had become Alice Ander's lifeline over the last two weeks. Her dad was home—thank you, God—but under doctor's orders to take things slow for the next twelve weeks. His therapist was scheduled to come to the house every day. Alice was glad of it—she was committed to seeing her dad get better. Terry Anders would live to keep on fighting—and keep on training fighters.

She heard laughter and turned to watch a group of teenagers leaving her dad's gym. Alice sighed. They were the only source of income for the whole camp at the moment. Picking up the unopened mail, she carried it into the kitchen and poured herself a glass of iced tea. She headed into the sunroom off the back of the main cabin.

She was glad to be back in the mountains and out of the city. Nestled in the Cascade Mountains in Oregon, Gilson was a small town of around five hundred people, close enough to several other small towns to ensure the training camps never lacked for visitors.

She sat in her favorite rocking chair and began sorting through the mail. She tossed the ads into the trash, stacked the bills in one pile and correspondence in another. On the bottom she found a letter from the hospital. Confused, she opened the letter and felt the blood drain from her face.

Insurance coverage terminated. Patient responsible for these charges. The statement asked for thirty thousand dollars! That couldn't be right.

Pulling her cell phone from her pocket, she dialed the insurance company and got through the automated voice recording and endless menu before connecting her with a live person.

She took a calming breath, her eyes straying back to the explanation at the bottom of the bill. Pinching the bridge of her nose, she took a breath and held it while she counted to ten. She heard a voice come on the line.

"My name is Alice Anders and I'm calling about a bill I just received for my father's recent hospital stay. It says his insurance coverage had been terminated?"

"Ma'am, if you could please provide me with your father's information, I'd be happy to check into this for you."

Alice gave the woman the required information, hanging up the phone some fifteen minutes later and feeling like her world had just ended. According to the insurance company, her father had been notified in March that as of July first, his current insurance plan would no longer be active and he'd need to choose another plan or have his coverage terminated. Her father had never contacted them, and as promised—or threatened—he no longer had insurance.

The woman Alice had spoken to had offered to email her the documents that needed completing to begin his coverage again, but it wouldn't start until September first. Too little, and way too late!

Tears burned Alice's eyes as she went through their options. They didn't have anywhere close to that kind of money in the bank, and her father's only income came from training fighters and the small monthly fees the locals paid for gym access. This could cost dad his camp—and that meant he wouldn't have a reason to get better.

She'd been planning to start her master's program the next week, but with her father's second stroke, the university had pushed her start date back until January. The grants and funds she had been awarded had been placed on hold as well. *If I get a job, can I even come close to earning this kind of money in four months?* She didn't know.

She was saved from more worry when Marguerite, her friend and neighbor and also their only help at the camp came to find her. "Hey, Alice, the fighter who called the other day—Bryant. He's shown up. Uninvited!" Marguerite sounded ready to take on the task of getting rid of him. And she could. Built like a bulldog, she somehow managed to make pearls at her neck and lace trim on her plaid shirt work. She also made regular use of the gym and was Alice's sparring partner. She hung in the doorway, waiting for Alice to give the word.

"What? But Dad's…" She trailed off as a crazy idea flashed in her brain.

Dad's ill, but I know how he trains fighters. I could train this guy for a few weeks and then send him on his way. At ten thousand a week, we'd be out of the woods in no time.

The idea was ludicrous, but as she headed into the house, she caught her reflection in the hallway mirror. She had always looked a lot like her dad—both of them tall and skinny. She had her dad's strong bones and more muscle on her than curves. She could work a bikini if she had to but she was just at home in sweats. *If I wore a cap and baggy clothes, no one would ever have to know. It's just Anders training the guy!*

She cocked her head to the side and envisioned herself wearing a cap, with her auburn hair tucked up beneath it, and pulled low over her eyes. She'd wear some of her father's long board shorts or his sweats, that would work for her. She'd tape her hands and flatten out her breasts with her tightest sports bra. She could wear oversize T-shirts and more sweats.

Think of the money!

"Alice, what do you want me to tell him?" Marguerite asked, pausing to watch Alice, a calculating look in her dark eyes. "What are you thinking in that head of yours?"

"Marguerite, I need your help. A bill came in the mail today for Dad's hospital stay. His insurance cancelled in July and we have to pay it all. I know how to train these guys as well as Dad does. But no one's going to pay the big bucks unless it's Anders *himself* overseeing their conditioning. I'm going to have to be dad for a short time."

Marguerite shook her head. "This is absurd! Pass yourself off as a man? Alice, please do not do this. There has to be another way."

Alice shook her head. "If Dad isn't training fighters, the camp isn't bringing in anywhere close to enough money to pay his bills. He's going to lose this place. We're going to lose him!"

Alice turned back to look in the mirror once more. Marguerite approached her from behind and gathered her hair up and pulled it behind her head. After several seconds of looking at her reflection, Alice met the housekeeper's eyes in the mirror.

"Thank God your father doesn't have any wrinkles. I suppose if you lower your voice… and wear some cologne."

Hope filled Alice's voice. "And all of those media days he had skipped. There have never been any close up photos of him online! Will you help me? If you treat me like I'm Anders—the Anders— that's going to help sell it to everyone." Alice looked at her reflection and quickly realized that even without mascara and eye shadow, she'd have to wear sunglasses most of the time as well. Either that or keep the brim of a hat pulled down lower over her forehead. She judged that her sculpted eyebrows and long lashes would be enough to give away her secret.

Marguerite dropped her hair and stepped away. "May God forgive me for aiding you in this foolishness, but I will help you. For your father. Tell me what you need me to do."

Grab your copy of *The Fighter's Fierce Temptation* (The Burton Brothers Series Book One) from www.LeslieNorthBooks.com

9 798231 998722